Daniel McClintock
McClintocks 4

By

Caroline Clemmons
Poems By Bea Tifton

Daniel McClintock
McClintocks 4

By

Caroline Clemmons

ISBN-13: 978-1985244153

ISBN-10: 1985244152

Copyright © 2018 by Caroline Clemmons

All rights reserved. Without limiting the rights under copyright reserved above, no part of this publication may be reproduced, stored in or introduced into a retrieval system or transmitted in any form or by any means (electronic, mechanical, photocopying, recording, or otherwise) without the prior written permission of both the copyright owner and the above publisher of this book.

Names, characters, places, and incidents are either the product of the author's imagination or are used fictitiously. Any resemblance to actual persons living or dead, businesses, events, or locales is purely coincidental.

DANIEL MCCLINTOCK

Chapter One

April 1888, Amsterdam, Holland

Clara Van Hoosan stood while her Aunt Petra measured her hem, all Clara lacked to prepare for her trip to Texas. Normally she would have measured from one of her other dresses, but she wanted this one to be perfect. She braced herself for her aunt's usual caustic comments.

Petra didn't disappoint. "Of course, if you were not built like a Viking, fitting your clothes would be easier and less expensive. And, your large bust over a small waist makes you appear out of proportion, as if you're going to topple forward."

Clara had heard herself compared to a Viking before. Long ago she'd learned to hide the sting of those words and of others even more unflattering. She couldn't help being almost six feet tall any more than she could change her blue eyes or blond hair.

She almost giggled because she *could* change her hair color but had no wish to do so. A giggle would provoke a reprimand from her aunt, so she kept silent. And, seeing as Aunt Petra was almost flat-chested, Clara believed the last comment was pure envy.

"I will soon be out of your way, Aunt Petra."

"You must know you are not in my way, Clara. I worry because I am not certain you should go so far away from your home."

Surprise at her aunt's almost-nice remark caused Clara to wobble. "I am excited about traveling to America. Not the sea voyage but the railway across the country all the way to Texas."

"Be still. The trip will be exhausting." Her aunt inserted one last pin and stood. "The Eerkens will see you to Chicago, but then you must find someone to act as chaperone to Texas. A young woman alone is prey to wicked men."

"I doubt a woman my size will be accosted, Aunt Petra. You said yourself I look like a Viking. Surely that's protection enough."

Her aunt's dark eyes sparked with anger. "Do not think this is humorous. You should do as I say. Hans and I have cared for you these twelve years since your parents' death. You owe us gratitude and respect. You would have been sent to an orphanage if we were not so kind."

As Clara had been reminded almost daily. She knew it was her uncle who had insisted she live with them against her aunt's wishes. Although she had never admitted that she knew, she couldn't overlook that fact.

"That is true and I am grateful that you allowed me to live with you. In addition to my brief nursing course, I have learned much from Uncle Hans that will serve me all my working life."

Her aunt stood with her hands at her waist and huffed. "And what have you to say to me, you ungrateful girl?"

"Of course I am grateful to you as well, Aunt Petra. You have taught me a great many things also—to sew, to cook, to clean, to host a party or a ladies' tea."

Her aunt had, but with Clara as a servant, not as an equal or beloved family member. Still, who knows what horrid conditions she might have faced in an orphanage? And, those skills she'd learned were bound to be useful all her life.

Her aunt gave her a searing glance. "See that you remember all you have learned, Clara. Now you had best finish this hem so the dress will be ready for you to wear on your journey. I am preparing some of your favorite foods for dinner."

"Thank you, Aunt Petra. I will finish before bedtime."

Petra gave a dismissive wave. "Why you agreed to go is beyond me. A young woman nursing and caring for a young man is not suitable. You are ruining any chance you might have had of making a good marriage."

"I have trained in mechanotherapy with Uncle Hans and his colleagues and I have completed the nursing course. I am well educated in all I will need in order to work with the boy in Texas. Helping patients is more important to me than whether or not a man believes I am suitable for marriage."

Her aunt stabbed the air with her forefinger. "So you think now. You will rue the day you agreed to this arrangement. You have no idea of living conditions and may find yourself in a terrible situation. I have heard the people in Texas are not even civilized. They carry guns and there is lawlessness."

Clara took a deep breath and bit back the retort she longed to make. "Please, Aunt Petra, I do not wish us to have harsh words on my last evening here."

Her aunt's clenched jaw relaxed enough for her to speak. "Very well, you are making your bed and will have to lie in it, for Hans and I cannot afford to send you the return fare."

"I intend to make a success there and do not expect to ever return to Amsterdam."

Petra gave a toss of her head. "Harrumph. The Eerkens will be here at eight in the morning to collect you and your trunks. Make sure you are ready."

"I will be." She gathered up her dress, careful not to dislodge any pins.

How she looked forward to being away from this oppressive home even though she was not especially fond of the Eerkens. Uncle Hans was always kind, but living with Aunt Petra was a daily test of good humor and patience. Surely Clara could control her temper for what was left of her time here.

In her little room upstairs she could hardly walk for the trunks and a valise. She had wondered why she was assigned what was undoubtedly intended as a servant's room when there was a suitable guest room a floor below and they never had houseguests. In one more day, this would not matter. She sat by the lone, small window to sew the hem of the dress she would wear tomorrow. Most things were packed with only a few stored in her valise.

She gazed at the first trunk, the largest, which contained her disassembled mechanotherapy equipment. The bars would need reassembly but she knew how. The second trunk held more of her equipment. In the smallest trunk, which was stacked atop the largest, were her clothes, her few possessions, and her mementos.

From her pocket, she pulled the letter that served as a contract. How lucky she was. The McClintock family lived on a ranch near a town called McClintock Falls. Perhaps the town was named for one of their ancestors.

Thank goodness they would provide her a room and her food and a salary that seemed huge. She wondered if they lived in one of the log cabins she had read about in America. Would they have many rooms or a small home?

According to what was written here, she would have her own room and eat meals with the family. Surely the room would be no worse than this one in which she had lived since she was ten. She hoped the family members would be pleasant and not like prune-faced Aunt Petra.

Clara reread the words about the young man, Daniel, who had been paralyzed from the waist down after his horse fell and pinned his back against a rock. Her heart ached for him. His age was not given, but she pictured him as about fourteen.

Ach, he would probably resent her because she was a woman and only twenty-two. Soon she would prove she was good at her job. She had been told she was one of the best at this modern treatment method.

***

May 1888, McClintock Falls, Texas

Daniel McClintock pushed his brother away from him. "What the hell do you think you're doing?"

Josh batted aside Daniel's hand, grabbed his arm, and pulled him to a sitting position. "We're tired of you lying around like you have no other choice. Dallas and I are taking matters into our own hands."

Bitterness consumed Daniel. "Nothing can be done to change what I've become. Let go of me." He might not be able to walk, but his upper body was even stronger than when that bastard Bob Tyson had shot his horse, Scout.

Before Daniel could toss his brother Josh onto the floor, his cousin Dallas came into the room. He'd always looked up to Dallas and the man's appearance effectively kept Daniel's fists from bashing his brother.

Dallas gently moved Daniel's legs to dangle off the bed. "I think this would work better if we were all in our socks." He sat beside Daniel and removed his boots.

Josh did the same on Daniel's other side. "Yeah, then we'll all be the same height. Where are your socks, Daniel?"

He looked from one side to the other. "Why do you want to know?"

Dallas' eyes met Daniel's. "Now don't get riled. We have a plan to help you. It may not work, but there's no harm in trying, is there?"

Somewhat placated, Daniel gestured to a chest across the room. "Socks are in the top drawer on the right."

Josh rummaged and held up a heavy wool pair their sister Rebecca had knitted. "These ought to work." He knelt and put them on Daniel's feet then sat beside him again.

Dallas pulled what looked like bandages from his pocket. "We came up with this idea last night, Daniel. Since Lance Clayton left for medical school, we figure you aren't getting enough attention. This won't be hard on you and we hope it may get your legs used to supporting your body." He bound Daniel's leg nearest him to his up to the knee.

Puzzled, Daniel watched his cousin. "There was no point in Lance postponing his training any longer. He was nice to delay as long as he did. He'll make a good doctor."

Josh copied Dallas' action with the leg next to him then tied a loop of the bandage loosely around Daniel's waist. "Now, sling your arms around our necks. When we stand, you'll come with us. We'll move our feet as if you were walking."

Dallas tapped the bandage at Daniel's middle. "If you get tired and start to fall, I'll grab the loop around your waist to haul you up so you don't hit the floor."

Fat chance. Daniel crossed his arms. "Listen, if you two think I'm going to parade around the house and grounds wearing a nightshirt and what amounts to a-a diaper, you're crazy."

Josh pulled Daniel's arm around his shoulder. "Won't anyone know what you're wearing under your nightshirt but we figured we'd stay in this room today."

Dallas looped Daniel's other arm around his neck. "On three we stand. One... two... three."

The other two men stood and Daniel was propelled up with them. Each one walked and doing so forced him to do the same. This was a crazy scheme, but he had to admit—hard as hanging on was—

being upright sure buoyed his spirits.

"I appreciate you coming up with this plan, but how is this going to improve my paralysis?"

Josh snorted. "Anything is better than wallowing in that bed every day."

"I don't wallow. I lay there and read or nap except when I'm in that dratted Bath wheelchair keeping records for Papa or painting."

Dallas said, "Your mind gets plenty of exercise. This is a workout for your legs. I know Aunt Kathryn massages your legs every day. Walking, even like this, lets your brain know how your legs are supposed to move and support your body."

He doubted this would make a difference. "I guess, if you say so."

His cousin sent him a glare. "I didn't say it would work overnight. Still, it's bound to help in the long run. Josh and I plan on stopping by every day and walking with you."

"With me? You make it sound like we're taking a stroll across the ranch."

Josh elbowed him in the ribs. "We will eventually. For now we're wearing out the floor inside. Get a handle on that attitude, will you?"

"Hell, I'm doing the best I can. How would you feel being useless for two years? I know you saved my life, Josh, but I almost wish I'd died when Scout did."

Dallas stopped walking and grabbed the front of Daniel's nightshirt. His face reddened and his eyes shot sparks. "Don't you ever say that again. Ornery as you are, you are precious to Aunt Kathryn and Uncle Austin. Times I wonder why but your kin and friends are fond of you as well. Do you think we'd stop grieving if you'd died? No, we'd never get over the loss."

Josh hung his head. "Much as I hate to, I agree with Dallas. We plan for you to recover, but even if you never do, you have a purpose. You save Papa from those infernal records he hates. You talk to us and share our time. You paint good pictures whose proceeds you donate to the church. And, believe me, they sell immediately. Why would you say such a hateful thing in the first place?"

Remorse settled on his shoulders. "Because that's how I feel sometimes. I can't sleep because I haven't done anything to tire myself.

Even though my legs don't work, they hurt as if they'd climbed a mountain slope. Doc says I have ghost pain and even amputees have the same problem."

When they turned, his mother stood in the doorway with her fingers against her mouth. Seeing tears in her eyes chopped through him like an axe.

She lowered her hand. "Watching you walk is wonderful, Daniel. I know you'll be walking on your own in the near future."

Daniel forced himself to smile at her. "These two think they're miracle workers. Maybe they are. Right now, though, I'm tuckered out."

They sat on his bed. Dallas pulled out his pocket watch. "Fifteen minutes. Not bad for the first try." He unwrapped their legs.

On the other side, Josh did the same. "You leaving on the socks?"

Daniel shrugged. "Might as well. Doesn't hurt anything."

Dallas and Josh maneuvered him to the correct position in his bed. Having their help drove home how helpless he was. In spite of what his cousin and brother had said, he doubted he'd ever walk again. He sank onto his pillow, dreading a lifetime of living in this bed, in this room, or in that blasted wheelchair.

Josh kissed his mother on the cheek. "Have to hurry home now. With Nettie so near time to deliver, I'm afraid to be gone long."

Dallas kissed his aunt's cheek. "Cenora sends her love. She'll stop by soon with the children. I'll be back same time tomorrow."

Kathryn hugged each man. "Thank you, boys. This means a lot to me. I'm sure it does to Daniel too."

When the two had gone, she poured Daniel a glass of water. "Did that tire you too much?"

"Naw." But he couldn't have been more worn out if he'd run a couple of miles.

She gazed at the window. "I see Doc Sullivan coming up the walk. I'll go let him in."

A few minutes later the chuckling doctor entered his room. "I hear you've been getting some exercise."

"That's right, against my will but I guess it didn't hurt anything."

"I have good news for you. I told you about the new treatment called mechanotherapy and the man named Van Hoosan coming from

Amsterdam. Well, I had a telegram today and he's set to arrive on Monday afternoon. I'll meet the train and bring him here."

He had to admit this was good news. Even if the man didn't help him, his presence would be a distraction. "Thanks, Doc. He's had a long journey. Coming here from Amsterdam means a ship fare plus the train and meals."

Daniel shook his head. "Damn, I have to tell you again I sure hate my folks have been out the cost."

"Son, your father told me he would do anything to help you. In his place, you would too. This Van Hoosan chap is trying to establish his name and hopes to found a practice in America. Isn't costing as much as you might think, the fare and room and board plus a very small salary is all."

Daniel gestured around him. "Plus they built on two rooms. Don't forget that took supplies and meant workers were tied up here instead of working on the ranch. Still, this room is large and has a nice view from the windows. The one next door looks pretty nice, too."

"Yep, not as luxurious as upstairs, but right pleasant. Van Hoosan will be quite comfortable and only has to step from one room to the other to see you. He'll be able to hear you call if you need help."

Daniel tried not to let hope build. After all this time, he was afraid there was nothing that would help him. Still, maybe this fellow could make a difference.

"Thanks for all you've done, Doc. Without your research we wouldn't know about this new kind of treatment."

"You're more than welcome. Now, let me check your lungs and heart. Can't let you develop pneumonia."

Chapter Two

Clara looked forward to parting with the Eerkens. When the train pulled into the Chicago station, Mrs. Eerken stared out the window. "There they are." She knocked on the window and waved. "Yoo Hoo, here we are."

"They can't possibly hear you." Her husband pulled her away from the window to help her stand. "You can talk to them when we get off the train. Do you have everything?"

She quickly gathered up a half dozen bags containing miscellaneous items Clara thought should have been packed into luggage. "I am ready. Clara, do you have your valise and purse?"

Clara wished she could snap at the woman but she held in her irritation. "I have."

They exited the train to the smell of steam and smoke. Soon they were surrounded by the waiting family—son Franz along with his wife and three children. Surprisingly, the children appeared normal and not winged angels as she had been led to believe.

When introductions had been completed, Mrs. Eerken took Clara's arm. "You remember how to find a companion for the rest of your trip?"

She nodded. "I have the agency ad in my purse. First, I will go to the hotel. I see the taxis lined up for passengers."

Mr. Eerken shifted from one foot to the other. "You are sure you do not need me to help you?"

She knew he asked only from duty and was eager to go to his son's home. "I will be fine. I only have to go to the taxi and give him the name of the hotel. My trunks are being forwarded to Texas by the rail line. Do not keep your family waiting on my account."

Mrs. Eerken said, "We will walk with you to the cab and make sure he knows not to cheat you."

"If you wish then why do we not hurry? I am sure your family is eager to get you to their home."

When Franz asked where she planned to stay, he shook his head. "That is a very expensive hotel. I know a less costly one that is suitable."

"You are more familiar with places in Chicago." Clara didn't mind taking his advice. He seemed nice.

Franz explained about American tipping on the way to the taxi. He helped her into the cab and gave the driver the name of the hotel he'd suggested.

When the horse was pulling the taxi away, Clara waved at the Eerkens. She was not sad to part with them but she was struck at how alone she was in a strange place. Part of her was excited to be on her own and another part of her frightened and wary. She had heard of tricksters who preyed on strangers, particularly foreigners.

The hotel recommended by Franz was one he said was modest in price. He might think so, but she was surprised at how much money each night's stay cost. If this was less expensive than her original choice, she was glad he interceded.

When she had finished checking in, she was assigned a room on the second floor—except it was called the third floor here. Already there were new things to learn. In America, the ground floor was called the first floor.

The clerk gestured to the right where she saw columns framing a large doorway. "Our dining room is open from seven in the morning until ten in the evening. You'll find we serve excellent meals." He snapped his fingers and a porter appeared. "Show Miss Van Hoosan to room 322."

She allowed the porter to carry her valise and followed him. This was the first time she had been inside a hotel and she tried not to gawk. Their steps made no sound on the thick burgundy and gold carpet. Dark gold-colored wall paper had filigrees embossed in a lighter shade.

The porter opened the door for her. "Here you are, Miss."

"Thank you." She remembered to tip him but she did not see why. She could have carried her own valise and easily have found the room without him.

When he had gone, she locked the door and examined the room. At the window, she peered out at the street below and the buildings across the way. Chicago was nothing like Amsterdam or any of the other cities she had seen on this trip. She had learned there was a large lake here, but she could not see water. No canals either.

Clara sat on the burgundy bed cover and counted her money. Her purse was never out of her sight on the trip. She had been warned of pickpockets who could take your money without you even feeling their touch.

Her money was safe. She was safe. Tomorrow she would board the train for Texas.

"*Thank you, Heavenly Father.*"

While she had searched in her purse, the advertisement for the agency had fallen out. She tossed it into the trash receptacle. A traveling companion was neither wanted nor needed. Quiet and solitude were what she desired.

Her stomach rumbled. "Well, Clara Van Hoosan, woman of the world, the dining room awaits you. And you can dine without Mrs. Eerken's constant chatter."

***

Days later, Clara stared out the train window. Seeing the landscape across America had fascinated her at first. She still enjoyed the changing view, but she was tired of riding the train. Walking on firm ground and sleeping in her own room would be welcome. Thank goodness, soon she would arrive at her destination.

The conductor walked down the aisle. "McClintock Falls, next stop. Coming up on McClintock Falls."

Her stomach roiled and she swallowed bile and fear. She used her handkerchief to dry clammy hands before she donned her gloves. After smoothing her skirt, she grasped her purse and valise as the train came to a halt.

Too late, she debated the wisdom of using C. R. Van Hoosan instead of admitting to being a woman. What if they didn't accept her? What would she do?

The contract!—she had a contract with Mr. Austin McClintock to work with his son, Daniel. Thank goodness. A dozen possibilities went through her mind.

She might be in trouble, but she would brazen her way. No, not brazen, just be strong. Smile, but be firm.

Dear Lord, please help me. Guide my lips and actions.

Gathering her courage, she exited the rail car. Only three others debarked when she did. She spotted her trunks loaded onto a cart being wheeled toward a depot.

The town appeared neat and she spotted several stores and a saloon. The visible streets were unpaved. Her nose itched when dust swirled behind a passing wagon pulled by two mules. People walked back and forth on the boardwalk in front of the stores.

Where was Doctor Sullivan? He'd promised to meet the train. She peered around, searching for someone distinguished-looking.

A gray-haired man wearing a brown suit and black string tie hesitantly approached her. He carried a hat, but not one of the wide types worn by most of the men she'd seen the last couple of days. His round face held a puzzled expression.

She forced herself to smile. "Could you be Dr. Sullivan?"

Eyes wide, he nodded slowly, as if he couldn't believe she was the person who'd come to help his patient. "Then you… you… are C. R. Van Hoosan?"

"I am, indeed."

His frown worried her. "Don't know how your patient will take to having a woman work on him."

Reassurances were called for—and fast. "I assure you there is no need for concern. I am a qualified heilgymnast and very good at using mechanotherapy to help those with paralysis."

The doctor rubbed his chin. "I'm sure you are, as you came highly recommended. We were expecting a man."

Her heart pounded. "Are you telling me you don't intend to take me to the McClintock ranch?"

"Not at all." He smiled and extended his hand. "If you'll give me your luggage claim slip I'll have your case loaded into my buggy."

She sighed and her knees threatened to give way in relief. "Thank you, Doctor Sullivan. The two large brown trunks and the smaller black one are mine." She retrieved the cardboard stubs from her purse and gave them to the physician.

An expression of surprise spread across his face. "You have three trunks? Well, of course you would, coming all this way."

"Two large ones for my equipment and one a bit smaller for my clothes and personal things. You see, I hope to make my way here in

Texas and don't intend to return to Amsterdam."

He cupped her elbow. "We'd better leave them here and send one of the McClintock cowboys in with a wagon. Don't know what I was thinking. There's no way to load three trunks onto my two-person buggy. I'll take your valise, though."

She looked over her shoulder where the cart had stopped. "But, will the trunks be safe simply left here?"

The doctor waved at a man near the railway ticket window. "Al Norris is the stationmaster. He'll keep them safe in the depot storage. Here we are, Miss Van Hoosan." He stopped at a black buggy then helped her up onto the seat.

Running her hand over the soft leather, she appreciated having a deluxe ride to her new home—if the patient would let her stay. Contract or not, he might refuse to let her near him.

When the doctor was beside her, she glanced his way. "Tell me about Daniel."

"Before the accident, he was a bit shy, polite, good-natured, and hard working. He's smart as a whip. Paints so well you'd think his work should hang in a museum."

He shook his head. "Sorry to say he's given up hope, become moody, and often snaps at people. He'll likely bite your head off, so be prepared."

"Oh, I am, for no one enjoys being infirm. I'll win his confidence, though it may take a few days, even a month. You have my promise I'll not give up."

"Thank you. The McClintocks are fine people. You'll never meet better. Daniel didn't deserve this to happen."

"No one does, but accidents occur. Repairing the damage is my job. That is, when there is nothing more a physician can do."

His brow furrowed and he shook his head. "I've done my best, but my best isn't enough."

"Tell me about the family? Is Daniel an only child?"

"His older brother Josh is married to an English girl. Sister Rebecca is about sixteen. Dallas, his cousin, came to live with the family when he was twelve because his parents were killed. I'd say Dallas is late twenties but pushing thirty. He's half Cherokee Indian has an Irish wife and two children. He's like an older brother to Josh, Daniel, and

Rebecca. The parents treat the four of them the same, and that's with lots of love and firm discipline. As I said, you won't find a better family anywhere than the McClintocks."

The doctor kept the conversation going on the ride to the ranch, pointing out businesses and homes. She nodded and made what she hoped were appropriate comments but she could not have repeated what any of the places were. Inside, her stomach was in knots and ropes constricted her chest. She fought to breathe without gasping.

Dear Lord, please soften their hearts so they won't turn me away. Bless my mind and my hands that I may help this young man. Again, Lord, thank You for this chance. Amen.

They turned up a tree-lined road toward a large, rambling, two-story home. A white exterior had gray shutters and white rails along the porch. Flowers bloomed in front of neat shrubs and a rose garden was at the side. Near the roses, a white gazebo invited visitors to sit on a bench inside. The welcoming appearance reminded her of a rambling story-book house.

She suppressed a gasp of pleasure that this was where she would be living for a while. The contrast between her uncle's narrow, three-story residence and the McClintock's emphasized the difference in life styles between here and Amsterdam. In fact, nothing here resembled her former life.

No cobbled streets with market stalls. No towering and ornate old buildings. No sailboats on the sea or canal.

Instead, endless land stretched to the horizon. Rolling pastures were broken by occasional woods. The only water in view was a river over which spanned a steel and wooden bridge.

Clara was encouraged. Surely with so many changes she could forge her life as a mechanotherapist even though she was female. In this land of opportunity, she would have a chance to accomplish her dreams. Time with her new patient would prove her ability.

Dr. Sullivan drew the horse to a stop. He climbed down and came around to help her.

"Sorry, I was staring at my surroundings instead of paying attention. I can get down by myself."

"Nonsense. You're a lady and must allow me to help you, Miss Van Hoosan."

She felt a blush spread across her face. Seldom had she been treated as a genteel woman. "Please, call me Clara. I'm sure we will work together to help Daniel."

The doctor carried her valise. "All right, Clara, let's go meet the McClintock family."

Clara's stomach housed a flock of fluttering butterflies. The urge to turn and flee struck her. Instead, she pasted on a smile and hoped she'd be accepted.

At the open door stood a beautiful woman and a handsome man who looked to be in their forties. Over their wide smiles their eyes held question. They stepped back so she and the doctor could enter.

Doctor Sullivan guided her into the house. "Kathryn, Austin, allow me to present Miss Clara Van Hoosan, a trained mechanotherapist ready to help Daniel."

Kathryn was first to react. "Welcome to our home. Let me show you to your room."

Clara held up her hand. "First, I must talk to the family without Daniel present. Will that be possible now?"

Austin wore a frown but gestured to the large parlor. "Certainly. Come right in here and have a seat." In spite of his facial expression, his voice held no censure but welcomed her.

Kathryn smiled. "I'll get our daughter. I'm sure she's hidden in some nook with her nose in a book. Oh, and I'll send in Emma."

Clara sat in a wingback chair near the fireplace. No fire was burning, but she sensed this would be a cozy room in cold weather. Furnishings suited this environment, from the leather couch and matching chair to the floor's braided rug.

Kathryn returned accompanied by two women. "This is Emma Harper, our housekeeper and cook who is like family to us. And this is our daughter, Rebecca, who's sixteen."

"I'm pleased to meet both of you. Mrs. McClintock, your daughter looks very much like you."

Austin still appeared concerned. "To tell the truth, Miss Van Hoosan, we were expecting a man."

"I realize that now but I assure you I am fully qualified and have several years' experience with great success." She met the gaze of each person in the room.

"Please call me Clara. I want to warn you that your son's treatments will be hard for him and I am sure he will resist having a strange woman tell him what he is to do. In my experience, I have had patients yell rude things when they begin but we come to terms and I win their confidence."

Rebecca's gentle laugh set her blue eyes sparkling. "My brother is grumpy as an old bear so I don't envy you. He's a good man, though, so please don't judge him by the way he acts now."

Austin leaned forward in his chair. "You can understand how frustrated he is, going from doing all kinds of physical labor to being condemned to his bed."

"Ja, I mean yes, I certainly do. Why I wanted to speak to you privately is to tell you that you are always welcome to watch us work. However, please do not intercede if he yells at me or I yell back. He needs to vent his anger at his situation and at me for forcing him to change. Please ignore anything he or I say during his treatments."

Kathryn glanced at her husband before meeting Clara's gaze. "We have placed our trust in you, Clara, based on the recommendation of John—Dr. Sullivan. He's assured us that this new method has had good results in Amsterdam and throughout Northwestern Europe and that you were labeled the best student of Dr. Von Breda."

Dr. Sullivan smiled. "Thank you, Kathryn. You know I've done a lot of reading about this new type of treatment. I truly believe this young woman can help Daniel."

Clara exhaled, relieved the family was open to her request. "I have had success, but it is not overnight."

Emma asked, "Have you eaten? We've had supper but there's plenty if you're hungry."

"I ate on the train, but thank you." In truth, she'd been too nervous to swallow any food. "I do need someone to collect my trunks from the rail station."

Kathryn stood and gestured toward a hallway. "We built on two rooms, one for Daniel and one next door for you. Let me show you where you'll be staying so you can freshen up if you wish."

Clara retrieved her valise. "Gladly, but I am eager to meet Daniel."

She followed Kathryn while Rebecca trailed behind. Her hostess opened a door and led them inside a large room.

"Since we expected a man, this is too plain for you but we'll make some changes."

Clara turned slowly, amazed that this large space was only for her use. "This is wonderful. I love having wide windows at the front. And the bed looks comfortable."

Wouldn't they be surprised to learn how bleak her old room had been with its dark gray walls, tiny window, and narrow cot?

Kathryn scooped up the quilt from the bed and handed it to her daughter. "Exchange this with the quilt from the pink guest room." When her daughter had left, she said, "A woman as lovely as you deserves a feminine décor."

Her hostess' words warmed Clara's heart. "You are being very kind. I was so afraid you would turn me out after you learned I am a woman. I assure you that I am well-trained and have had success with my patients—once they get over the fact I am a female."

"I understand. I'm an herbal healer and midwife. I face discrimination myself. Some never get over their mistrust, including my mother-in-law." A look of alarm came over Kathryn. "I have no idea what came over me to say that."

Clara smiled. "I did not hear a thing except that you are a healer and midwife. What a wonderful profession. No wonder you have been able to help your son as the doctor said."

Kathryn's eyes filled with pain and unshed tears. "I've done everything I know but it hasn't been enough. At least his legs haven't withered as you might suspect after two years."

"May I meet him now or do you prefer I wait until morning?"

The other woman twisted a handkerchief she'd pulled from her pocket. "No, I think you might as well get acquainted now."

Dr. Sullivan picked up his hat. "I'll be going but I'll check in to see how the therapy is progressing."

Clara turned toward the doctor. "Thank you again for everything."

Her hosts added their goodbyes then Austin excused himself to give her luggage claim cards to someone named Red.

Kathryn laid her hand on Clara's arm. "Please be patient. He was such a kind, sweet young man before the accident. I know he will be again if only he can walk once more."

Clara smiled, hoping she would reassure the boy's mother. "That is why I am here, Mrs. McClintock. I will do everything I can to make that happen."

"Please, call me Kathryn and my husband Austin. I imagine we'll be like family before this is over."

"Thank you, Kathryn. I suspect you are right, especially since I am living under your roof."

Kathryn dabbed her eyes with her handkerchief. "Daniel has been so depressed he won't even argue."

Clara chuckled. "I imagine that will change when he meets me."

She clasped her hands in front of her. "Shall we visit your son?"

Chapter Three

Clara followed Kathryn to the room next door. When she entered, she stopped and stared. Daniel wasn't a boy as she had imagined—he was a man her age or older. And, as handsome as any man she'd ever met.

Kathryn introduced them to one another.

"You're not serious!" Daniel's glare chilled Clara as he assessed her head to toe and back up. "You said a man was arriving. You think I'm going to work with this… woman?"

He looked away and made a dismissive wave with his hand. "Forget it and get her out of here."

Kathryn offered Clara a helpless expression then left the room.

Clara stepped forward, forcing herself to assume her professional demeanor. She had faced this reaction before, but this was so much more important. As much as she longed to help anyone in his position, this man also represented her chance to establish herself in America.

"Daniel, I am here to help you learn to walk again. I have a contract and have moved into the room next door, so you might as well get used to having me here."

His blue eyes were glacial. "I. Said. Get. Out."

As if he hadn't spoken, she continued, "I have completed courses in nursing, and mechanotherapy and have helped dozens of people like you recover the use of their limbs. One of your workers has gone to the rail depot to claim my trunks. Inside two of them I have equipment which I will assemble here in your room."

He threw a book at her but it landed at her feet. "I am not letting you near me."

She picked up the book, glanced at the title. "Hmm, *Tom Sawyer* by Mark Twain. I have wanted to read this. Thank you." She laid it on the washstand.

"Give me my damned book."

She smiled but didn't return the tome. "But, you gave it to me."

"You know very well I didn't." Using his arms and hands, he pushed up higher on his pillows. "You deliberately misled us by using your initials instead of your first name."

She widened her eyes and blinked at him. "Oh? I believe it is customary to use initials in business correspondence."

He crossed his arms over his chest. "Don't give me that innocent expression. You knew we thought you were a man—which is what you intended. I'm not having a woman working on me."

Clara tapped a finger against her cheek. "I was under the impression your mother has been working with you to insure your leg muscles do not deteriorate. You were not averse to her and she is a woman."

"That's different."

"She faces prejudice because she is a woman healer. I would think you, as her son who is aware of this, would be more tolerant of other women healers."

"What she does is entirely different than what you supposedly do."

"Not so. Each of us does our best to help people. In spite of your low opinion of me, I am going to be helping you for some time. I will be in early tomorrow to help you get ready for the day. After breakfast, I will begin assembling my equipment. You will find it fascinating. For now, good evening." She reclaimed the book and carried it with her.

He yelled after her, "Bring me back my damned book!"

She smiled to herself as she walked to her room. She thought she had come out best in that round. Tomorrow would begin round two.

***

Daniel beat his fists against the bed. Bad enough to have his body hold him captive but he was not going to have that woman work on him. He shuddered when he imagined the humiliation of her changing his diaper. As if having to wear one wasn't bad enough.

No way in hell was he submitting to such degradation!

She'd have to leave and that was that. Served her right for deceiving them. That story that using her initials was "customary in business correspondence" was nonsense. She'd misrepresented herself intentionally because she knew a woman would never be hired for her position, especially a woman so young. He'd bet she was younger than him.

If she was so good at her job, why leave Amsterdam? Yeah, why did she want to come all this way across the world when she was supposedly successful there? He'd ask her if she dared come back into this room.

And she had better return his damned book.

***

In the master bedroom that night, Austin took off his boots. "What do you think of Clara? I admit I have reservations."

His wife pulled her nightgown over her head. He watched as the fabric fell around her, covering her nakedness. Never would he forget how lucky he was to have his wonderful Kathryn return his love and marry him.

She adjusted the garment's ribbons at her neck. "She comes with excellent references and talks as if she knows what she's doing. Dr. Von Breda wrote John that he was sending his best student. We should accept her and see how Daniel improves."

"You mean *if* he improves." He fisted his hands. "I wish I could wring Bob Tyson's neck."

Kathryn hugged him. "Don't say that. Tyson's gone and we have to be here for our boy."

She leaned her head against his chest. "I've done everything I know and it's not enough. I get so frustrated and despondent that I can't help crying sometimes."

Austin held her against him but didn't admit he was often so discouraged that he had cried over the past two years. "He's only twenty-two. What if he never improves? What kind of life will he have?"

His wife kissed his cheek. "I can't say why, but I feel Clara will help him. At least, let's give her a chance. What else can we do?"

"You're right, Love. But, if Clara fails, we've run out of ideas. John stressed that this method she uses is gaining world-wide recognition."

He ran his fingers through his hair. "I worry about Daniel's mind. He's grown so despondent and out of sorts. Not that I blame him, but how can we help him get rid of that attitude?"

"If he relearns to walk—or even improves a little, his outlook will change. I'm sure he will. Oh, Austin, I'm counting so much on this young woman's ability."

"I know, Love, I know. As you said, what else can we do?" He caressed her back in small circles then steered her toward their bed. "Now, let me show you what a waste of time it was for you to pull on that nightgown."

***

The next morning, Clara dressed carefully. For therapy work, she wore a white muslin split skirt and shirtwaist without a corset. The ensemble allowed her the flexibility needed to work with a patient.

She hurried to check on Daniel. He lay on his back, staring at the ceiling. Glancing around the room, she saw numerous paintings. She recognized the ranch's landscape in three. Others showed horses, two alone and two in groups.

"Good morning, Daniel. Dr. Sullivan mentioned you paint well and I see he was correct." She walked the length of the room and back, admiring the lovely paintings. "These are beautiful."

"They're for Roan's store to sell and donate the money to the church."

"Shall I help you get ready for the day?" She reached for his sheet.

He batted away her hand. "Don't think you're going to be helping me. You run along and do whatever it is women do each morning."

"*This* woman helps you. I hoped you would reconsider after thinking overnight. We can do this peacefully or in an all-out war, but I will help you."

He screwed up his face and mocked, "'I vill helf you'. You can't even speak proper English."

She raised an eyebrow. "I am sure my English is far better than your Dutch."

"Are you so eager to see a man's privates that you're willing to help me? Does ogling a man intimately get you all hot and bothered?"

She fanned her throat and pretended to pant. "Oh, yes, I just adore looking at piss and feces." With one yank, she snapped the sheet from atop him.

"Hey, you... you can't do that."

"I already have." After pouring water into the pitcher, she wrung out a clean wash cloth and carried it and the towel to his bed. She grabbed one of the clean cloths used as his diapers.

He scooted up on his pillows and put out a hand. "Get away, do you hear?"

"How could I not? I am sure men working in the barn heard you. You may as well save your breath. We will start your bath with your face."

He grabbed the wash cloth from her. "I can wash myself."

"If you wish." When he'd cleaned his face and torso, she rolled him to lie on his chest and washed his back and pulled the covering from his posterior.

"Hey, what are you doing?"

"Checking your skin. Your mother has done a wonderful job of preventing bedsores. There is one tiny area on each of your hips where tissue has changed."

"You said there weren't any bedsores."

"That is right, but these places must be watched carefully or there will be. Now that you will be moving more, that should help."

She touched a scar low on his spine. "You are fortunate the rock damaged your spine so low. Otherwise I would not anticipate you regaining use of your legs but I do."

He craned his neck so he could look up at her. "Lady, if I were fortunate, I wouldn't be paralyzed in the first place."

"That is true and I am sorry you were injured. However, we must deal with your reality and not with wishes. In that way, you are fortunate."

Clara helped him turn to his back. She fought to be as impersonal as possible with the mantra taught her by her nursing supervisor. *Pretend he's a dish and you're cleaning the kitchen.*

She had never seen a dish this handsome, that was certain. She removed his pelvic covering. "I know you can do the front, but I need to check your skin this one time."

He turned his face to the wall but she could not help seeing his face's scarlet skin. She sympathized but could not let his embarrassment or hers prevent her from doing her job.

When he was once again covered and wearing a nightshirt, she washed his legs and feet. She scooted the wheeled Bath chair near his bed. "Are you ready to go into breakfast?"

Surprise registered on his face. "What? No, I eat in my room."

"Nonsense. You are part of your family and should eat with them. Besides, consider that you only make extra work for Emma when you eat in here." She lifted his arm and put her shoulder underneath then stood, easing him to the chair. He was heavy but she had been trained in lifting people.

"You are the most stubborn woman on earth. What don't you understand about me wanting to stay in here?"

"Not a thing." She covered his legs with a small knitted blanket then pushed the chair toward the kitchen.

When they reached the breakfast room, Emma almost dropped the platter she was carrying. Kathryn broke into a wide smile. Rebecca's eyes widened and she quickly added another place setting.

Austin clapped Daniel on the back. "Glad to see you joining us, Son."

"Didn't have much choice with this Viking maneuvering me."

Kathryn glared at him. "Son, you'll address Clara respectfully at our table or I'll pour your share of gravy on your head."

He looked down and muttered, "Yes, Mama."

Ignoring him, Clara took a seat. "Is not this a lovely morning? Thank you for the wonderful mattress and pleasant room. When I looked out the window of the room you assigned me, cheerful birds were eating breakfast in front of your house."

Kathryn passed her the bacon and ham. "I'm happy you slept well. A ranch is a bit noisy in the morning. Austin's already been working in the barn."

"I heard commotion, but it was a comfortable, reassuring sound."

Kathryn and Rebecca were dressed in colorful cotton dresses that flattered their coloring. They must think her cream muslin dress very plain and odd.

"I must explain my choice of clothing." She gestured at herself. "This is my work uniform. As you can see, this split skirt is more serviceable than attractive. Truthfully, it is a gym costume designed for women who ride bicycles but this is how the other women mechanotherapists dress."

Kathryn's smile appeared genuine. "You are dressed in a practical way. Too bad you don't have man-style pants to wear. That would be more appropriate for what you do."

"Yes, but I would create a scandal if I wore them. Perhaps someday in the future I will gather the courage to do so."

Rebecca set down her milk. "Tell us about your trip. Were you traveling on your own?"

She spread her hands on the table. "Oh, my travels were a grand adventure. From home I accompanied family friends, Mr. and Mrs. Eerken, to Chicago. My aunt intended me to find someone else to act as chaperone from there but I did not try. I enjoyed being on my own after being saddled with the Eerkens for that long."

She widened her eyes. "Um… not that they are… um, unpleasant people, but, frankly, they are boring unless you want to hear endlessly about the accomplishments of their children and grandchildren. I was tired of that subject long before we reached England."

"Weren't you afraid by yourself? I've heard a lot of criminals ride the train to rob people." Rebecca asked.

"If I were tiny and frail, I probably would have been scared. As noted, a woman who is built like a Viking is less tempting to con men and thieves."

Daniel coughed, and she guessed it was to cover a laugh.

"Looking through the rail car window was interesting. I had no idea there were so many kinds of terrain in America."

Austin set down his fork and leaned back. "What was the most unusual part of the journey?"

"Hmm, I suppose that would be crossing the Mississippi River. It's so wide and I was afraid the train would fall off the track or the bridge would crumble. When we reached land on the other side, you may believe I was relieved. Of course, I was asleep each night on the trip and may have missed something else spectacular."

Conversation changed to ranch matters and soon the meal had ended and people dispersed.

Clara wheeled Daniel toward his room. "Would you like to sit on the porch for a little while and enjoy the morning?"

"No, I want to go back to my room."

***

Daniel wondered how he could make this woman understand he preferred hiding away in his room. He certainly didn't want the men he'd worked with to see him this helpless. Better to let them forget he even existed.

Two large trunks waited in his room. So much for the men forgetting him. Two of the ranch hands must have had to deliver these.

Remorse weighed heavy on him. He longed to explode out of this wasted shell he'd become. A split second and his life had changed him from being happy to being useless.

Clara's cheerfully annoying voice pulled him from his reverie, "Are you going to sit in the chair and glower or would you prefer to scowl from your bed?"

He took over and used his hands to turn the wheels. She must think she was funny. "I'm tired so I'll return to bed."

"I will help, shall I?"

"Someone will have to and you're the only one paid to do so."

"I see the bed is pushed against the wall. I will be sure to move it so tomorrow you can get up on the right side for a change."

"Ha ha. You think you're funny, don't you?"

She plumped up his pillows and stacked them so he would be almost sitting up. "Even though you are not an admirer, some say I have a clever wit." She locked the chair's wheels and helped him to bed.

He sank onto the pillows. In truth he was exhausted simply from being up for half an hour.

"You had better rest while you can, Daniel. I am going to assemble the mechanical therapy system now."

She opened the largest trunk and lifted out a series of wooden and steel bars, chains, and pulleys as well as a small tool box. As though she'd done so a hundred times, she set about fitting together her equipment.

He watched her project grow. "Do you plan to use my entire room?"

"Yes, I will use the length. Do not worry because I will not touch that corner where you have your easel and paints. I know your brother and cousin have been visiting to work with you in here, but they can use my room."

"Has anyone told you you're a martinet?" She was also educated and intelligent. He couldn't prevent that from intimidating him.

Instead of getting mad enough to leave, she chuckled. "Only at first. Later, patients come to admire me."

"Believe me, that day will never come here."

She wagged her finger at him. "Never say never. You may have to eat those words."

His younger sister Rebecca came in and plopped on the foot of his bed. "What are all those?"

He answered before Clara could, "My torture devices."

Rebecca, the little traitor, giggled. "Funny, Daniel, but I suspect they're going to help you walk again. I meant what kind of devices."

Clara smiled at his friendly sister. "Rebecca, they are to help Daniel but it's going to be a hard-won battle. When I finish connecting all these properly, I'll give you a tour."

His sister tilted her head and studied Clara's work. "Looks hard to assemble."

Clara reached for a wrench then glanced quickly at him. He sensed she would like to hit his head with the tool.

"The hardest part is obtaining your brother's cooperation."

Rebecca punched his shoulder. "I'm sure he'll cooperate. Everyone in the family will yell at him otherwise."

Clara didn't look up from her work. "No need, I can yell loud enough for everyone."

He scowled at her. "Humph, I believe that." She was certainly stubborn and he'd bet she could shriek like a banshee when riled.

His sister giggled and stood. "This is entertaining but I don't see that me being here helps anyone. I'll go help Mama prepare her herbs and tinctures."

He watched Clara bending to set a screw in her nutty apparatus. He had to admit she had a fine figure. Not that it changed his objections to her being here.

"You put that together as if you've done so before."

She glanced up then went back to work. "Ja, I have. Uncle Hans insisted I practice in the gymnasium before I packed the pieces. Each one is numbered."

That caught his attention. "Gymnasium? I thought you worked in a clinic."

"We worked in a gymnasium because this is an athletic activity. I am called a heilgymnast as well as a mechanotherapist. You see, in this instance, *heil* means to heal and that makes me, like your mother, a healer."

"If you were so successful there, why did you agree to come here?"

She sighed and pushed a blond curl from her face. "Holland is a small country and that is primarily where this therapy originated. There are many heilgymnasts there, mostly men, and far more than the clientele can support. I thought in this new country which is so vast, eventually I would have the opportunity to establish my own clinic."

She stood and faced him. "Dr. Sullivan wrote that there is a great need here. He searched for ways to help you and found there was nothing to compare to the success we have had with this method in Amsterdam. He said absolutely nothing is in this area."

The sound of heavy boots approached. Laughing, two handsome men who must be Josh and Dallas came into the room.

Josh looked as if he'd been poleaxed. "Whoa, what's happened here?"

Dallas ran his fingers over one of the rails Clara had raised. "This is fine workmanship." He stepped forward and extended a hand to Clara. "Since my cousin isn't going to introduce us, allow me. I'm Dallas McClintock, and this fellow beside me is Daniel's brother, Josh."

Clara's face colored slightly. "I am happy to meet you both. Kathryn told me how much you have helped Daniel."

Josh recovered enough to smile. "With your permission, we'll get to work now."

Daniel used his thumb to point at his chest with a fist. "Her permission? What about mine?"

Josh waved his hand dismissively. "Aw, we know you don't agree so there's no point asking." He looked at Dallas. "Let's get this done."

Clara watched as the two positioned Daniel, sat on either side of him, wrapped legs, and stood. When they were walking out of the room, she clapped her hands. "This is wonderful. You will help teach his mind to make his legs work as they should. Oh, you are wonderful family members to think of this."

Daniel couldn't see behind him, but he heard her footsteps as she followed. Damned if he didn't feel like an exhibit in a science laboratory or museum. Since she had his room full of her equipment, they paraded through the downstairs.

Clara said, "You can walk in the room next door where I have my things. That's a large room."

Dallas slowly pivoted so Josh could make a wider turn. "Naw, we don't want to invade your private space. This is good."

Josh chuckled. "We're thinking of taking this show on the road. Might make some money on a tent exhibition."

With a smile, Dallas shook his head at his cousin. "Started out at fifteen minutes and now we're up to thirty."

Daniel was certain they'd walked for hours each time. If only his legs actually would support him. In spite of the enthusiasm of his cousin and brother, he couldn't tell any difference in feeling or movement since they'd started this experiment. Make that lack of feeling and movement. At least, hanging on was easier now.

Clara beamed at the trio. "I am excited to see this. What a clever arrangement you have."

Back and forth they walked.

When he could tolerate no more, he said, "Enough for today. I'm ready to drop. Can't hold on to you two much longer."

They returned to his room and sat on the mattress. When they'd unwrapped and stowed the bandages for another day, the other two men helped him lie down on his bed.

Dallas nodded at Clara. "My wife and children will be over to meet you soon. Houston, that's our two-year-old, has a cold so we're keeping both kids inside. I'll be back tomorrow, same time."

Josh pointed at Daniel. "Me, too. We're not stopping until you're running up and down the road."

He nodded at Clara. "Nice to meet you, Clara. My wife is expecting any moment and not leaving home now, but you'll meet her once the baby's here and she's up and about. In the meantime, you're welcome to come for a visit. See you tomorrow."

As soon as his kin had gone, Clara poured a large glass of water. "I imagine you are thirsty after all that walking."

"As if I've been out on the desert for a few days." He tipped up the glass and drank half then sipped the rest.

By the time he finished and set aside the goblet, she was back at work on her equipment but glanced up when he set down his glass. "Shall I pour you more?"

"Not now. Believe I'll have a short nap." He tried to roll to his side so he'd face the wall.

Before he realized it, she was beside him. She helped him change position and placed a pillow at his back to stop him from rolling. He'd missed having help since his former aide, Lance Clayton, had gone to medical school.

Mama, Emma, and Rebecca checked on him often, but it wasn't the same as having someone in his room all day. Maybe having Clara here wouldn't be so bad.

Naw, who was he kidding? Nothing she could do would help him.

Chapter Four

Daniel watched Clara as she finished assembling her infernal bars and something he couldn't identify. He refused to let her think he was dumb because he had lived in the country and gone to a tiny school. He'd show her he was as smart as she was.

"Did you know the giant squid can reach eighty feet long?"

Instead of appearing impressed, she laughed. "I am glad no one told me this before my sea journey. I would have been watching for long tentacles snaking over the ship's rails all the way."

"Are you about finished?"

She stood and smiled at him. "All is assembled and ready for you to use. This apparatus will help you learn to walk again."

"Not interested." He looked at the wall.

She made a little huffing noise. "You agreed to work with me. Your parents have gone to a great deal of expense and trouble to get me here and have these rooms built. Are you so selfish and self-destructive you will not even try?"

Anger surged through Daniel. "You know there's no hope. Why work myself into a sweat when it won't make a bit of difference? I put up with Dallas and Josh's antics because they don't give me a choice and at least it's a chance to visit with them. I have a choice in this."

She rested her fists on her hips. "Do you think so? You spineless baby. Shall I get Rebecca to bring you one of her old dolls so you can cuddle?"

"You've got a nerve talking to me that way. You lied to us, making us think you're a man. You know you wouldn't have been allowed to come if we'd known you're a woman."

"I explained that. One does not use full names in business correspondence. Would you prefer I sign Clara Roos Van Hoosan? Well, too bad. I am here and I am the one working with you." She clutched his hand. "Now get over your childish pout and cooperate. Every day you waste means your parents are paying me for nothing."

He frowned at her. "Roos is a funny name for anyone."

"Roos means rose in English and was my mother's name."

She had assembled the bars, anchored to the floor with permission from his father to drill into the floor. From higher rails, an overhead harness would allow Daniel to be suspended with his feet on the floor. With his hands on the waist high bars, he could propel himself along. His feet would drag but he couldn't fall.

"I will be in front of you and move your feet as if you are walking. At the end of the bars, the harness can pivot so you can reverse direction.

"How is that more effective than what Dallas and Josh had devised?"

"We can work here for longer periods—as long as my knees and hips do not protest too much. Dallas and Josh can only devote so much time to helping you."

His anger didn't abate but he let her pull him so he sat on the edge of the bed with his feet hanging off. "They're paying you for nothing anyway. You know I'll never walk again. Why hold out that carrot when you know it's pointless?"

"Do not say that. Do not think that." Her facial expression emphasized her anger toward him was palpable. She hooked something around him. "This is a harness so you cannot fall. Do you understand you will be safe?"

"I told you I don't want to do this. You are the most stubborn woman I've ever met."

"Then we are a pair because you are the most stubborn man I have ever treated. I do not care whether or not you wish to do so, you will exercise and you will learn to walk." She pulled his arm around her neck and guided him between the parallel bars.

He didn't exactly bounce but the harness moved with him. "This feels weird. What if the support breaks and I fall? How do you expect this to work?"

She squatted in front of him. "You move your hands forward on the rails as I move your feet. Don't worry, you will not fall."

"I feel like I'm going to. How can you be sure this system will hold me?"

"Because we tested it on a man who weighed about twice what you do. Move your hands forward."

He stayed where he was, which meant his feet were ahead of him.

She sent him a searing stare so heated that it would ignite wood in a fireplace. "Move. Them. Now."

"All right, if you're going to be so gripey." He moved his hands ahead and gradually caught up with her. "What happens at the end of the bars?"

She glanced up but held his feet. "I told you. You turn around and we go the other way."

"Damn. How long do you intend to do this?"

"If you mean today, until my legs give out. This is not the most comfortable position. If you mean overall, until you can walk without holding the bars."

***

Clara sailed into Daniel's room. "Good morning. How are you today?"

"The same, how do I look? You're here early. Go away. I need to sleep another half hour."

"Not now."

"Not interested." He pulled up the sheet and closed his eyes.

She whipped the sheet from him. With him frowning at her, she got him washed and his clothing changed.

"Are you happy now? I was sleeping really well and having a good dream." He leaned against the pillows and closed his eyes.

"Spoiled baby, today you will learn to move from the bed to the chair by yourself."

His eyes popped open. "I'll fall."

"No you will not. I will be right beside you."

"So you can pick me up?"

"Now, Daniel, please use your hands to navigate to the edge of the bed with your back toward the chair seat."

"You're sure the wheels are locked?"

"Of course. No more stalling." She made a come here motion with her hand.

He hesitated. "If I fall I could ruin my back forever."

"You will not fall. I am right here. We have covered this. Get busy."

He looked doubtful. "You are a tyrant. I don't have to do what you say."

"You most certainly do have to do what I say, whiney baby. You are only wasting time and showing yourself a coward."

"You make me so mad, Clara Van Hoosan." He moved as she'd instructed.

"With your hands on the chair armrests, propel yourself onto the seat."

He did and released the brake to wheel away from the bed.

She grabbed the chair. "Don't move far, only until your heels are still on the bed but your legs are not. Lock the wheels again."

"This must look pretty stupid. Lock, unlock, lock."

"Why would you care? With your left hand gripping firmly on the left arm rest, reach your right hand forward and lift your right leg to the chair support. Don't let your heel drop against the wood or you might bruise or scrape the skin."

"Maybe I should have worn socks."

"Perhaps. Repeat with the other foot."

In spite of his complaining, when he had completed the maneuver his beaming smile announced he was pleased with himself.

"You plan on making me do your work, do you?"

She laughed. "If I can, why would I not?"

"I think you delight in torturing me."

"Yes, that is my main source of pleasure. Now, time for breakfast." Clara wheeled him to the kitchen.

Clara parked Daniel and took her place at the table. "Breakfast here is a cheerful and pleasant meal."

Kathryn passed the bowl of scrambled eggs. "Your aunt and uncle weren't talkative in the mornings?"

Before she thought, Clara admitted, "Aunt Petra was never cheerful but even less so in the morning. I suppose Uncle Hans had grown used to not speaking early in the day. Most meals were solemn and quiet."

Rebecca asked, "What happened to your parents and how old were you?"

Kathryn hissed, "Rebecca!"

Clara smiled. "Please, I do not mind anyone's questions. In Rebecca's place I would be curious. I was ten when my parents died. A horse attacked my mother. When Papa tried to rescue her, he was killed. The horse had to be put down because it was crazed and impossible to train."

Austin's blue eyes held sympathy. "I'm glad you had kin to take you in even if your aunt wasn't a happy person."

Clara looked from him to Kathryn, unwilling to reveal how unwanted she'd been. "You took in Dallas, yet you treat him as if he were your son. That is especially kind of you."

Kathryn laid a hand on Clara's arm. "We love him as if he were our son. His parents were wonderful people. His maternal grandfather, John Tall Trees, has moved here to be near him, his wife Cenora, and their children. Dallas is half Cherokee Indian, which is why his grandfather has such an unusual name."

Austin pointed his fork at Clara. "You'll meet my parents tomorrow evening when they come to dine." He pointed the fork at Daniel. "And you'll be respectful to Gran."

Daniel gaped at his dad. "When have I not been respectful?"

His father speared him with a glare. "That means eating at the table when my parents are here."

Daniel turned to Clara. "Prepare yourself for an inquisition."

Clara smiled at those around her. "I am sure that after living with Aunt Petra, your Gran will not distress me."

Rebecca shook her head. "You only say that because you haven't met Gran."

***

The next evening, Clara dressed carefully. After so many weeks of travel, she was out of condition. Her shoulders ached from her time working with Daniel. She wished someone would give her a massage. Briefly, she wondered if Kathryn would do so.

Admittedly, Clara was wary of meeting the older woman who so intimidated this lovely family. Even Daniel, who did not even like Clara, had warned her. She sighed. Probably Gran was no worse than Aunt Petra.

She wore her pale gold embossed satin dress and a burgundy jacket because it was the finest ensemble she owned. In Amsterdam, she had worn it to church and to dinners and had received many compliments. She did not wear any jewelry except a locket that had been her mother's, which she fastened around her neck.

In addition, she gathered four small gifts she'd brought with her. Handkerchiefs were not elaborate, but they were necessary for ladies. She hadn't anything for the men.

When she was dressed, she went next door to make certain Daniel was ready to be wheeled into the parlor. He wore the clothes she had laid out for him and waited in the Bath chair.

"My, how nice to see you dressed."

He looked down at his clothing. "Pa helped me with the pants. I- In case I have an a-accident, I intend to use that lap robe Rebecca knitted." He appeared to assess her. "You look nice."

"Thank you." Clara unfolded the small blanket and tucked it around Daniel's lap and legs. "You'll probably be too warm with the covering."

"Too bad if I am. Damn, I hear them in the parlor." He took a deep breath, as if bracing himself. "We could just wait in here and I'll plead an upset stomach. To tell the truth, seeing Gran makes me so nervous she gives me stomach cramps."

"You are not allowed to play the coward, Daniel McClintock. You are lucky to have grandparents and must at least be civil and respectful."

He leaned back to look up at her. "Grandpa is really nice. I used to be able to get away with the men and leave Gran to fuss at Mama and Rebecca. Now I can't escape so easily."

Clara tucked her small packages beside Daniel and wheeled his chair into the parlor. A distinguished-looking couple waited with Austin, Kathryn, and Rebecca. The older man had gray hair and smile lines creased his face. His blue eyes twinkled and she saw the resemblance to Austin and Daniel. Beside him, a stately woman in the latest fashions had gray hair and a face scrunched in disapproval.

Austin stood and gestured toward them. "Ah, isn't seeing Daniel dressed and able to come into the parlor wonderful?"

Austin came toward them and stood beside Clara. "Mother, Papa, may I present Miss Clara Van Hoosan, formerly of Amsterdam, Holland? Clara, this is my mother Zarelda McClintock, who we call Gran, and my father, Victor McClintock, who we call Grandpa.

Clara nodded to each of the newcomers and tried her best to enunciate English properly. "I am very pleased to meet you."

Gran narrowed her eyes at Clara. "You've come a long way. Did you travel alone?"

"My aunt did not believe that would be proper. Family friends accompanied me most of the way."

"What on earth possessed you to go into such an occupation? Surely you don't intend to pursue it permanently?"

Inside, Clara bristled in annoyance but she retained her smile. "I chose mechanotherapy and being a heilgymnast because it allows me to help people like Daniel. To answer your other question, I intend this to be my life's work and would like to one day have my own clinic here in America for those with paralysis." She understood why Daniel and Rebecca had warned her.

Grandpa squeezed his wife's arm. "Lucky for us you were willing to travel here to help our grandson. We're grateful."

Gran frowned but made no other comment.

Clara reclaimed her gifts and carried one to Gran. "Please accept a small token from me."

Gran's eyes rounded as she accepted. "Why…why… thank you."

While Gran opened her present, Clara handed one to Kathryn and another to Rebecca. "I appreciate the generous welcome you've given me."

Kathryn's face lit with pleasure. "How nice of you when we're so happy you're here."

Rebecca tore open the paper. "Oh, what lovely handkerchiefs. And there're three of them. Thank you." She stood and hugged Clara.

Standing with the remaining package was awkward.

"Please excuse me while I give this to Emma." She slipped into the kitchen and gave the last gift to Emma.

The housekeeper's face shone. "For me? How kind of you, Clara."

When Clara returned to the parlor, Austin and his father exchanged information about ranching and various ranchers in the county. Kathryn asked Gran about social events in town. Rebecca went to the kitchen until she called everyone to dinner.

Usually, the family ate at the large oak table in the kitchen. Clara loved the friendly, casual atmosphere. For the first time since her arrival, they gathered around the formal dining table. One chair had been removed to allow Daniel's chair access to his place.

She regarded Gran's elaborate lilac taffeta gown and amethyst and diamond jewelry. The elder McClintocks must be very wealthy. Clara's dress, which she had formerly thought to be lovely, appeared shabby beside Gran's.

Kathryn and Rebecca were dressed well, but not as ostentatiously as Gran was. Clara was relieved the two women she admired were not overdressed. Members of the McClintock family were so attractive, however, Clara would be a house sparrow by comparison no matter what she was wearing.

She was seated between Daniel and his grandfather. Gran sat directly across the table from Grandpa. Clara sensed the older woman scrutinizing her with disapproval but pretended to be oblivious. Kathryn sat next to Gran.

Emma brought platters and bowls for them to dine family style. Rebecca helped the cook/housekeeper then sat by her mother. At every other meal, Emma had eaten with them. Apparently she was not doing so this evening. Clara longed to slip into the kitchen with Emma.

After grace, dishes were passed and conversation flowed with trivial matters. When they were finishing dessert, Gran started in on Clara—just as Daniel had predicted.

"Young woman, how old are you?"

"Twenty-two." Clara wanted to ask Gran the same question but bit her tongue instead.

Gran waved a hand in the air, making a circle. "How is it you're supposed to be this medical wizardess when you're so young?"

Clara laid down her fork. "I finished school at sixteen then began my training. I began working with patients under supervision when I was eighteen. On my own, I've been treating patients as a heilgymnast for over two years with great success."

Gran tapped her fingernail on the table. "I don't hold with that foreign talk. Speak English, girl. What does that heil...whatever you said mean?"

"The word 'heil' has several meanings, but in this instance it means 'heal'. The word 'gymnast' is coupled with 'heil' because healing is done in a gymnasium-like setting. Loosely translated, 'heilgymnast' means 'healing therapist' and the method I use is called 'mechanotherapy'."

Gran's eyes widened. "I declare, not another make-believe healer? This family collects them like a hound dog collects fleas." Her mouth turned down in what looked like a perpetual pout.

Grandpa leaned forward. "Zarelda! Miss Van Hoosan is here at the request of Kathryn and Austin through John Sullivan."

Daniel set down his glass. "Gran, you shouldn't insult Mama or talk to or about Clara that way. Do you want me to be an invalid for the rest of my life? You think there's something wrong with having someone with special training work with me? Do you remember that Clara was recruited by Dr. Sullivan after much investigation?"

Gran sent a searing glare to Daniel. "Of course I want you walking again. I can't see how this woman is the answer. Weren't you expecting a man?"

Clara laid a restraining hand on Daniel's arm then quickly pulled back when she realized what she'd done. "Mrs. McClintock, there was confusion and the family thought a man was arriving. However, I was chosen specifically because I have had experience with patients suffering from the same type of paralysis as Daniel's and achieved a high rate of success. I assure you I am adequately equipped to assist your grandson in learning to walk once more if anyone can. And, I truly believe he will walk again."

Grandpa smiled. "That's good news, Miss Van Hoosan."

Gran harrumphed. "Still, not a proper job for a woman."

Kathryn scooted back her chair and stood. "Why don't we go into the parlor?"

Austin quickly rose and helped his mother with her chair then escorted her to the parlor.

Daniel announced, "I hope you'll excuse me. I'm tired from all the work Clara had me doing today. Good evening." He peered at Clara. "I'll need your help."

Grateful to escape even though he didn't need her, Clara grabbed the handles and wheeled his chair toward his room. "Nice to have met you, Mr. and Mrs. McClintock. Good night."

When the two of them were in Daniel's room, she closed the

door. He removed his shirt and vest and pulled on his nightshirt. After Clara had helped him onto his bed, she tugged his pants from his legs.

When he was tucked in for the night, she stood beside his bed, hands on her hips. "I have two things to tell you before I say goodnight. One, there is no need to defend me. I am perfectly able to speak up for myself. Besides, your grandmother is not as fierce as you believe."

His scowl changed his handsome face, but didn't wipe away his good looks. "What makes you think that speech was for your sake? You think I appreciate having Gran come to our home and act as if she's Queen Zarelda and we're all far beneath her? She shouldn't have been so rude to you because it reflects on Mama and Pa. I intend to point that out to her whenever she acts that way around me."

He shook his head. "You should have heard some of the things she's said to Mama about her healing." He inhaled deeply. "So, what's the other thing?"

She smiled at him, hoping it softened her features. "Two is thank you, Daniel. Even though—or maybe especially—because it wasn't necessary, I appreciate your support. I'm not accustomed to having someone defend me."

She took a breath. "Do you want the lamp out or do you plan to read for a while?"

"Leave it." He reached for his book without meeting her gaze. "I'll read for an hour so."

"Good night." She went to her room.

She readied for bed, surprised at how Daniel had come to her assistance. His grandmother was a mean-spirited harridan for certain. His grandfather was a sweet man. How in the world did those two come to be married this long?

That reminded her of kind Uncle Hans and acidic Aunt Petra. There were strange couples who made her question the likelihood of their marriages. Perhaps there was even a man for her somewhere.

Chapter Five

In their home that night, Victor McClintock sent a stern gaze at his wife. "You were rude to that young woman and by inference, to Kathryn. How long are you going to carry this hatred for Kathryn?"

"I don't hate her. Only Austin could have married well. If he'd chosen Marla King as I urged him to do, he'd have acquired a fortune and social standing. Instead, he chose that so-called healer with no family and nothing to her name. What a waste!"

"You think Josh, Daniel, and Rebecca are a waste?"

"Of course not. Except for Daniel being paralyzed."

"Austin chose Kathryn because he loves her. He didn't need someone else's fortune—he's acquired one for himself. You have to stop this, Zarelda. All these years Kathryn has been a wonderful daughter to us. She's helped hundreds with her herbs and delivered dozens of babies. You know John Sullivan calls on her for help at times. Why can't you accept that she is the woman for Austin and good at what she does?"

As if she hadn't heard him, his wife gazed at an unknown point in the room. "I wanted the best for our boys. Houston had to go and marry that heathen woman and get killed. If he'd been here, that wouldn't have happened. Then Austin married Kathryn."

"You don't know what life Houston would have had if he'd been here. Do I have to remind you that if you'd accepted Gentle Dove, then Houston would have lived here near us?"

She snapped, "You do not. Please don't mention it again."

Seeing the pain in her eyes, he changed the subject to the here and now. "We couldn't have a better daughter-in-law than Kathryn. She's a good wife, good mother, good healer, and good to us in spite of the way you treat her. Why do you persist in mistreating her?"

"Drying plants and giving them to people is not the way a proper lady acts. Nor is working as a... whatever this young woman called herself."

"I don't remember the term, but she comes highly recommended. Who says that's not proper for a lady? You think people would be better served if Kathryn and Clara deserted their patients and sat around drinking tea and gossiping? Maybe like Viola Ruthson, who ran away with her husband's best friend? She was a lady, wasn't she, and a member of your ladies group?"

Zarelda gasped. "Don't mention that woman's name. She fooled us but her true nature showed."

He took his wife by her shoulders. "You promised me you'd do better. For some reason I love you but I'm not above revealing details about your father's embezzling and prison sentence."

Fear shadowed tears in her eyes. "No, please, don't tell anyone. You promised. I'll… I'll try to put aside my reservations and be more accepting."

Gently, he kissed away her tears. "We've had a tiring day. Let's turn in and see what tomorrow brings."

"I love you, Vincent. I know I don't deserve a man like you, but I'm so grateful you're my husband."

He hugged her shoulders. "Me, too, Love. Me, too."

***

Whenever one of the cowboys went into town, he collected mail for everyone at the ranch. One day, Kathryn handed Clara a letter from the stack of envelopes and packages.

"This is from Aunt Petra. I am surprised she is writing to me." She opened the letter and sank to a chair. "Oh, no."

Kathryn touched Clara's shoulder. "Do you have bad news?"

"Uncle Hans had a heart attack the week after I left and he's… he's dead." With her eyes filling with tears she kept reading the letter. "I will read it aloud, but it will be slowly while I translate in my head."

Clara,

My Hans died from a heart attack the week after you left. You will receive a letter from the solicitor telling you what happened to the money from your parents' home and farm. This should have come to us because we took you in for all those years but Hans planned for you to have the proceeds. We were arguing about this when his heart gave out. This makes my grief worse. I am all alone now and lost.

You sound as if you are in a good place with kind people. I envy you.

Your Aunt Petra

Kathryn hugged her shoulders. "I'm so sorry. I know you were fond of your uncle."

"Ja, he was my mother's older brother and always good to me. Not Petra, she deserves to feel lonely and lost."

Clara laid a hand against her cheek and gasped. "What am I saying? I am ashamed I had such a petty thought when my aunt is grieving too."

Kathryn shook her head. "That reaction was shock speaking. I know you are too kind to mean that. From what you've said, though, your aunt doesn't instill good thoughts."

"She had a circle of ladies there but I believe they were the wives of other men from the university. Now Petra will have lost what she had in common with them. She may truly be lonely."

Clara reread the brief letter. "I will write her tonight and send my condolences."

***

The next morning, Dr. Sullivan came to check Daniel. "You're improving, young man. Your pulse is stronger and your lungs sound clear. Obviously, Clara's routines are beneficial."

Daniel glanced at her before training his gaze on the doctor. "Don't encourage her, Doc. Already she works me to half to death. Josh and Dallas still come every weekday and drag me around."

The doctor nodded. "Hmm, I'll bet you're sleeping better now, aren't you?"

Clara wanted to laugh at the mixture of emotions playing across Daniel's face.

He finally admitted, "Yeah, I've been sleeping six hours straight every night. I'm grateful for that even if nothing else works."

She stepped forward. "You will walk again." She shook her finger at him. "Do not doubt this. Believing really does help recovery. If you are positive, you send messages to your brain and there is an unconscious response."

Daniel rolled his eyes. "Malarkey. Horse feathers."

The doctor returned his stethoscope to his bag. "She's right. You know I read a lot of medical journals and papers. There are many case studies that prove this is valid. Never give up, Daniel."

A skeptical expression settled on Daniel's face. "If you say so, Doc. I'll admit I had resigned myself to never leaving this room until you told me Clara was on her way here."

Daniel laughed and a twinkle sparkled in his blue eyes. "No, not her. A Mr. C. R. Van Hoosan, I believe."

Clara sighed. "I suppose I'll never hear the end of that even though I explained that signature form is common in business correspondence."

Dr. Sullivan picked up his bag. "Good to see you on the upswing. I'll see myself out."

Rebecca sailed into the room, graceful as a swan. "Any chance of stealing you, Clara, to go horseback riding?"

Blood pounded in her ears and her breath caught in her throat. She had to clear her throat with a cough. "Thank you, but after what happened to my parents I stay clear of horses. Perhaps we can do something else soon, like take a walk or quilt or something that doesn't involve huge animals."

Laughing, Rebecca waved and left the room.

Daniel studied Clara. "Afraid of a horse? I'm surprised. Didn't think you feared anything."

Shrugging, she straightened his cover then poured him a glass of water.

He took the glass but didn't raise it to his lips. "What? No witty comment to vindicate yourself?"

"I am not ashamed to admit my fear of horses. You know my parents were killed by a crazed horse. What you don't know is that I watched from the corral fence."

Daniel set the glass on the bedside table. "I'm sorry. That must have been horrendous. How old were you?"

"Ten. Mama admired a magnificent chestnut stallion in our neighbor's field. The neighbor, Mr. de Graaf, warned my parents that the horse had never been ridden and had a wild nature. That only increased Mama's desire to have the horse—I admit she was strong-willed and spoiled."

Daniel's eyes widened. "Surely she didn't try to ride him?"

She shrugged. "She intended to. Papa and the neighbor saddled him and Papa was going to ride first. They were all three in Mr. de Graaf's small corral. At the last moment, Mama argued that she wanted to be the first to ride the horse. She and Papa argued, their voices grew loud and Mr. de Graaf tried to intervene. Mama actually yelled at him and pushed away his hand."

Clara covered her eyes with her hands, as if she could block out the memory seared into her mind. "Suddenly, the horse pulled his halter reins from Mr. de Graaf and attacked Mama. When Papa tried to rescue her, the horse stomped him, too."

Daniel's wide eyes filled with sympathy. "And you saw this happen?"

Saddened at the reminder, she nodded. "Yes, all of it. When the neighbor got the stallion under control, Papa was dead from a crushed skull and Mama was badly injured. She died a few days later."

Not before she told Clara goodbye and asked for forgiveness. Her beautiful mother couldn't bear knowing she'd caused the death of her beloved husband.

Daniel's voice snapped her out of her assault of memories. "Then you went to live with your aunt and uncle?"

She crossed her arms over her chest and turned to face the window. "Ja, yes. They didn't know I'd heard Aunt Petra argue against taking me to live with them. She wanted me sent to an orphanage. Uncle Hans put down his foot because I was his only sister's only child. Dreading being taken where I wasn't wanted and totally lost without my parents, I packed my things and a few mementos and went to live in the city of Amsterdam. I suppose Uncle Hans disposed of the farm and the household things."

His voice held a note of humor. "Aha, but you were initially a country girl. Perhaps our ranch doesn't seem too remote then."

"I enjoy being here, even when you're cantankerous which, as far as I can determine, is constantly." She turned to face him. "Your ranch is so much larger than our little place. Papa grew tulips but we had a couple of good horses he and Mama rode for pleasure. Occasionally, Mama would take me riding. Our other stock was for farming or eating—plow horses, pigs, a milk cow, and chickens."

"You had a nice life there?"

She found the courage to smile. "Very nice, but if I had remained in our little village I would have had no opportunity to learn after I was sixteen. Other than Papa, no one I knew went to university. It was a simple life, but I was contented. I believe Mama wished for more, but she loved Papa and never urged him to leave the farm he so enjoyed."

"What do you think she wanted to do?"

Clara sighed. "I don't know. When she and I were alone, she sometimes spoke to me of theater and large shops and fancy parties with a faraway look. She grew up in Amsterdam and I think was quite sought after by beaus. While she didn't attend university, she had attended a ladies seminary. Aunt Petra had nothing after she finished public school."

"Odd how things work out, isn't it? No wonder your aunt was jealous of you. But, I'll bet your aunt misses you."

She grinned at him. "Do you think so? I've wondered. I helped her with the housework so I thought she might miss having me do that, but she never acted as if she even liked me."

Clara threw up her hands. "What am I thinking, standing here yammering about my past? You must have a nap and we will continue treatment afterward."

"A nap doesn't sound bad. You pummeled me pretty hard this morning."

"Think so? Wait until after your nap." She left him to rest and went to the kitchen for a cup of tea.

***

Several nights later, Clara was in bed, tossing and turning instead of sleeping. She was so hot she considered getting up and replacing her nightgown with her chemise. Would that be too scandalous? How could people sleep in this heat?

A loud bang from the next room was accompanied by, "Damn, damn, damn!"

She leapt up and grabbed her lamp. After lighting it, she rushed to Daniel's room. He was lying on the floor between his bed and her equipment.

She set down the lamp and knelt beside him. "What happened?"

"I thought I could lean far enough to reach the wheelchair and paint for a while. Obviously, I was wrong."

"Are you insane? You could have broken an arm and then you would be in trouble." She examined his arms and shoulders then his legs.

"Guess I was monkeying around." He frowned. "What are you doing dressed for winter sleeping?"

"This is my only nightgown, which a gentleman would pretend he has not seen."

He chuckled. "You already know I'm no gentleman. At least you don't have it buttoned up to your chin. When you lean over, I can see—"

She clasped the fabric together. "Never mind what you thought you could see. Sling your arm over my shoulder and I'll try to lift you onto the bed."

He did as she asked. "You should ask Rebecca to loan you something cooler."

She met his gaze. "Oh, and how would that conversation go? 'Your brother thought my nightgown looked too hot so he told me to borrow a cooler one from you.' That would be scandalous, would it not?"

He laughed. "I wish you would say that but only where I could watch her expression. On the other hand, you could simply tell her you're smothering in your only gown and ask if she can loan you one until you can go into town and purchase something cooler."

Using her legs, she was barely able to lift him from the floor onto his mattress. "This was harder than when you are in bed and I move you to the chair. Please do not fall again."

He held out his hands, turning them palm up and palm down. "No damage done I take it?"

"You may have a bruise on your buttocks by morning. Otherwise, I suppose you are all right."

"I meant to your back from lifting me."

"Oh. No damage that I can feel now but we will see tomorrow. Please stay in bed until I show up in the morning."

"Yes, Ma'am." He wiggled his shoulders to settle on his pillows.

"Goodnight… again." She returned to her room. This time she slept.

Chapter Six

After breakfast, Clara signaled to Rebecca to follow her to the hallway. "How long will the weather be this hot?"

Rebecca blinked at her. "Until mid September and maybe later. Our hottest weather will be in July and August. Why?"

"Our home in Amsterdam was very old and of thick stone. My room was always cold. The only nightgown I have is flannel and I've been uncomfortably warm at your home."

The other woman squeezed her arm. "Oh, Clara, you should have spoken sooner. You must have been miserable each night you've been here. I'll loan you one of mine if you don't mind wearing someone else's clothing."

Rebecca looked down at her chest then at Clara's. "On second thought, I don't think mine will fit. I'll check with Mama. She has a fuller... um, bosom than I do."

"Thank you. If someone is going into town soon, perhaps I could send money and ask that person to purchase one for me."

Rebecca laughed. "I can't see Red shopping for a woman's nightgown. Maybe if Mama put it on the list and Mrs. Roan wrapped it in brown paper he wouldn't know the difference. Perhaps we can go to town together soon. I'll ask Mama while you torture Daniel."

"Thank you." Clara returned to the kitchen to find Daniel had left. She went to his room and he sat waiting for her.

"Ah, you wheeled yourself. I hope that means you are feeling stronger and more empowered."

"Might just be boredom, you know? Truthfully, I hated being in Emma's way while you and Rebecca chatted. She gonna loan you cooler nightwear?"

Clara sensed her face color. "She thought hers might be too tight in the chest. She is going to consult your mother."

Daniel chortled. "Don't know why I didn't think of that. You are definitely more… um…" He used his hands to cup where breasts would be if he had them.

Clara waved her right hand. "Enough of that conversation. Time to get to work on your therapy."

After an hour and when he was even with his bed, Daniel stopped. "I don't know about you, but I'm exhausted."

She was grateful to stand. "All right, let's get you back on the bed and I'll give you a massage before your rest."

He did as she asked. "Do you know tigers have striped skin, not just striped fur?"

She paused. "I did not know that. I am not sure that knowledge will ever be useful."

"All knowledge is useful." A frown creased his handsome brow. "What do you do while I nap?"

She grinned at him. "Recover. Remember, I was the one duck walking while you rode in the harness."

An hour later, she left Daniel to his nap and went to her room to lie down for half an hour. On the bed was folded a lovely batiste nightgown trimmed with tiny tucks, soft lace, and blue ribbon. The garment was lovelier than any sleepwear she'd ever seen.

She ran her fingers over the fine, soft fabric. Never had she thought she would wear something so feminine and elegant. Tonight she would be cool enough to rest well.

***

That night, Daniel lay with his arm across his eyes. He might have given in to doing Clara's exercises, but he still hated having a woman witness his helplessness. Worst was having her change his damned diaper. He'd thought he'd die of shame the first time that happened.

Clara was like a general in the damned army. If she'd been in charge, the Civil War wouldn't have lasted more than a month. Hell, if she were in control, it wouldn't have happened at all. She'd have ordered the South not to secede.

His angry tirade against Clara was interrupted by a strange sensation. He pushed himself up on his pillows. Could that have been tingling in his big toes? Naw, probably what he'd felt was more of the ghost pain that plagued him.

Wait—there the sensation was again. He focused on moving his toes, carefully observing the sheet covering his feet. Sure enough, the fabric moved as he focused on his toes.

He wanted to laugh and cry and shout and scream all at once. He'd believed the work was pointless. Now his heart filled with hope. Maybe he would walk again after all.

***

The next day, Clara was massaging Daniel's legs. As if he were waving at her, his right big toe moved.

Elation filled her and she gripped his foot. "Daniel, did you move your toe intentionally?"

He grinned at her. "Had this tingling yesterday. Last night when I was thinking about the exercises, I was angry. I figured out how to move my big toe on each foot. Surprised the heck out of me."

After rushing to her tools, she found the instrument she wanted. "Tell me if you feel this." She ran the steel against the bottom of his foot."

"I feel that. Reckon that means I'm getting feeling back?"

She wanted to jump with joy but contented herself with smiling at him. "Yes, oh yes. I 'reckon' that is what this means. Congratulations."

He grinned at her. "Guess getting mad at you paid off."

"You have worked hard and I think that is the reason for your new ability. However, if being angry produces results, then I will try to make you angry each day."

"So far, you've been doing a good job of that."

She scoffed, "So you pretend but I know I am the soul of reason and could not possibly be the cause of your anger. I am excited with this progress."

He loosely grabbed her wrist. "Would you go tell Mama? She's worried so about me. Knowing I've made improvement will make her feel a lot better."

Clara started to leave then turned back. "Why do we not go together and you can show her. She deserves to see for herself."

He pondered for a few seconds. "I guess… if you think it's important."

"Ja, it is very important." She helped him into his Bath chair.

"This will indeed give her spirits a lift, as it has mine." She pushed his chair from the room.

They found Kathryn in the studio where she grew and stored plants and prepared her healing supplies. Apparently, Rebecca was assisting her. There was no spare space, but Clara parked her patient near the door where the other two women could see his feet.

"Daniel wants to show you something."

Each woman stared at Clara and Daniel expectantly.

Daniel wore a sheepish smile. "Watch my right foot." He wiggled his toe.

Kathryn and Rebecca grabbed one another and squealed in delight.

Clara beamed as if she had been the one to accomplish a great feat instead of him. She was pleased to see these two good people this happy. "I know that moving toes sounds only like a minor thing, but it means there is still some connection in his spine."

With tears running down her cheeks, Kathryn pulled a handkerchief from her pocket then used it to blot her face. "Thank You, God, for your mercy! I'm grateful to you, too, Clara. You've put in long hours to help Daniel."

Daniel held out his hands, palm up. "Isn't anyone going to give me any credit? I was working, too, you know?"

Kathryn rushed to hug her son. "I'm so proud of you. This is encouraging. Rebecca, go and tell Emma then go find your father. We'll go into the parlor where there's room for us."

Rebecca hurried toward the kitchen.

Immediately, a wide-eyed Emma came to stand by Daniel. She hugged him. "I said you would walk again someday. Now you can believe so too."

He patted the housekeeper's hand. "I hope we don't have to wait another two years."

Clara assured him. "It won't be. In two years, this will seem like a bad dream as you walk wherever you wish."

"On water?"

Clara punched his shoulder. "You are not Divine, Daniel McClintock. Since I'm standing close to you, I hope lightning doesn't strike you for your irreverence."

He tilted back his head to look at her. "Just kidding. I'll be pleased to walk across my bedroom."

Austin came jogging into the parlor with Rebecca. "Son, I came to see for myself."

Clara turned Daniel's chair so he faced his father. Daniel wiggled his toes.

Austin fell on his knees. "Thank You, God, for answering our prayers this far!"

When he raised his head, his eyes were moist. "Son, I can't tell you how happy I am."

He rose and pumped Clara's hand. "Thank you for your therapy."

Clara hated to dampen anyone's enthusiasm but she had to rein them back to Earth. "Daniel will still have a lot of work ahead. But, now that we know there is at least some connection between his mind and his lower extremities, perhaps he will not hate his exercises so much."

Daniel groaned. "You're a slave driver, Clara Van Hoosan. But you're right. I'm encouraged and you won't need a whip anymore."

"Oh, no, and I was going to order a new one to crack over your head."

Everyone laughed.

Laughing through her tears, Emma wiped her eyes with the corner of her apron. "This calls for a special supper tonight. I'll see what I can rustle up."

***

When Josh and Dallas came the next day both wore wide smiles. Clara helped Daniel sit up and position himself for his assistants.

Josh pulled the stash of bandages from where he'd stowed them in the chest drawer. "Heard you had a celebration last night. So good of you to invite us."

Daniel bumped shoulders with his brother. "Mama wanted to but I told her not to bother until I could walk. Moving my toes is not worth a family party."

Dallas clapped Daniel on the shoulder. "Sure is good news. Soon you'll be walking off and leaving us."

"Thank you both for your help. Clara says it's made a lot of difference. I know coming here inconveniences you."

Dallas grinned at him. "If it were one of us, would you be willing to help?"

"You know I would." Daniel's eyes widened and he reared back. "Okay, I see what you're saying. All the same, being my walkers eats into your day yet you've come every weekday."

Josh winked at Clara. "Yeah, you're probably not worth it, but we figured if we got out of a little work, why not?"

As the three men stood, Clara asked, "How is Nettie?" She followed them from the room.

When they went sideways to get the three through the doorway, Josh glanced at her and rolled his eyes. "Nettie swears she's going to explode and an elephant will emerge. We thought she would have had the baby by now. Doc says the first is often late."

"Aunt Kathryn checks on her daily. My aunt knows her business."

"Yeah, and Mama is saying Nettie is doing fine and the baby will come when things are right."

"Ja, some things cannot be hurried. I am sure Nettie is more than ready, especially in this heat."

The three men turned and Josh shot her a glance. "Worst of the heat isn't here yet. Her ankles are swelling, though, and Mama told her to rest a couple of hours each morning and in the hottest part of the afternoon."

Dallas nodded. "Cenora's ankles swelled a lot with baby Katie. Don't remember that being a problem with Houston."

Cenora sensed that Josh and Dallas were good husbands. When each spoke his wife's name, his voice held love. She was struck again by what a nice family the McClintocks were.

"Dallas, how old are your children?"

Humor tinged his voice. "Houston is two. Little Katie is four months. Houston's cold cleared but the baby caught it. We're keeping them home until they're both fit. Surely that will be soon."

Clara said, "I have heard that many small illnesses are the way with children but I believe they are worth every inconvenience."

Dallas grinned. "That they are."

***

Late the next evening, a giant man arrived during supper.

Kathryn leaped up from the table. "Grizzly, did you come for me?"

He held his hat at his chest. "Yes, Ma'am, Miz McClintock. Josh said you're to come right away."

Austin stood. "You get your bag and I'll hitch the horse to the buggy."

"I'll come with you, Mama." Rebecca scooped up the last bite of her pie.

When they'd gone, Clara asked, "Did Kathryn call that man Grizzly, like the bear?"

Daniel chuckled. "She did. His real name is Howard Pierson, but most cowboys have some nickname or the other their coworkers have given them."

"Soon you'll be an uncle and Rebecca an aunt. I suppose you already feel like one because of Dallas' children."

Austin returned near bedtime. "No news yet." He chuckled. "May have to send for the doc to treat Josh. Kathryn had to make him a cup of calming tea and make him lie down in the next room."

By bedtime, they'd had no word. Early the next morning, a cowboy knocked on the kitchen door.

Emma motioned him inside. "Come in, Lucky. Any news?"

"Josh said to tell you he has a boy named Austin Clayton McClintock. Mother and baby are doing well." He grinned. "Not sure Josh is okay."

Austin beamed. "Named him after me, did they? Well, I have to go see this boy." He clapped his hat on his head and left.

Chapter Seven

That night when he was alone, Daniel lay in bed staring at the ceiling. Beams from the full moon flooded his room. Light cast shadows and illuminated objects as bright as a lantern.

He was an uncle. He couldn't say why that had made such an impression on him. Damn! He knew why.

Josh wasn't that much older than him. Dallas and Cenora having children didn't make such an impact because Dallas was eight years older and someone he'd looked up to even before his cousin came to live with them.

Here he was stuck in this damned bed, celebrating because he could move his damned toes. Hell, like that was a big accomplishment. He held a pillow over his face so Clara next door wouldn't hear him sobbing.

He wanted his life back. Wanted to feel the wind on his face as he rode a horse across the pastures. Jump in the river with a splash and swim. Run up the stairs two at a time to his old room.

Letting the tears flow, he failed to hear the door open.

Clara pulled away the pillow and sat on the bed. She helped him sit up then cradled him against her shoulder.

As if he were a small child, she patted his back and soothed him. "Crying is good now. Let the anger and frustration flow from your body."

His voice caught in his throat and he coughed. "Here I am, crying like a five-year-old who skinned his knee. You must think me a whiney baby."

"No, no. We both know that your injury is far more serious than a skinned knee. Letting your feelings out does not mean you are weak or childish."

He'd never wanted anyone to see him like this, blubbering like a child, but he couldn't stop. "I've tried to be positive, tried not to dwell on the past. I can't help it. I want to be like I was."

"You are making progress. Do not lose hope now."

He took a deep breath. "Easy for you to say. You know I'll never be the same."

"You will still be Daniel, just as you are Daniel now. The outside is a shell." She leaned away and cupped his face in her hands. "I truly believe you will walk again. I do not lie and would not say this if it were not true."

He pulled away and wiped his eyes with his palms. "Like I was?"

She shook her head. "You are right that nothing will be as it was. You have lost years of your life that cannot be reclaimed. Nothing remains the same. You will be a new Daniel, perhaps better than before even though you may walk differently."

He moved his hands from his face. "What do you mean by 'differently'?"

"Probably you will not be able to run and you may even have an unusual gait. Still, you will be walking from place to place to do as you wish."

"Like ride a horse."

"I said walking but, perhaps, if your legs are strong enough to swing into the saddle then you can. You know how your weight distributes itself as you go through the motions of mounting a horse better than I do."

He beat the mattress with his fists. "If I can't ride, then I'll be stuck with nothing to do but Pa's record keeping."

"Nonsense. You are a grown man who is very intelligent and can do many things. You paint and keep finances. Who knows what else you will accomplish? There is far more to life than riding horses."

He shook his head. "Not for a rancher. This was supposed to be *my* ranch when Pa and Mama are gone. Dallas and Josh each have their own places. You think men would take orders from a cripple?"

She snapped, "Don't ever refer to yourself in that way. The only thing that will be crippled is your mind unless you stop. If you are going to mope and feel sorry for yourself, you can do so without me." She stood and would have left.

Daniel caught her hand. "No, don't go. Please." He guided her back to where she had been sitting.

"Why should I stay?"

He waited a few seconds to gather his courage before he replied. "I was thinking about Dallas' children and now Josh having a baby." He met her gaze. "I wondered if…if I'd ever be able to… um, father children?"

Sympathy tinged her soft voice. "Only time will tell and I cannot guarantee anything. In my experience, some men are not able to have normal intimate relations even though they regain use of their legs. Most who relearn to walk are, though."

"So, I have to wait to learn which group includes me. That's not helpful."

She laid her hand over his. "Daniel, you have worked hard. So have I and your mother before me. Josh and Dallas have done what they could, too. Dr. Sullivan—and your mother—prevented you from dying of pneumonia or heart problems, the diseases that usually attack paralytics. The young man, Lance, also helped you. You have excellent resources. But, I have been here only a few weeks. One cannot undo this much damage in so short a time."

"All right." He caught her fingers with his. "How long do you think it's going to take?"

She shrugged and shook her head slightly. "There is no way I can tell. I will do the very best I can to help you. I expect you to do your best too."

"I have been. If I don't walk again the reason will not be because I didn't do my part."

She smiled and smoothed hair off his forehead with her fingers. "Good. Can you sleep now?"

"Not without a goodnight kiss." He had no idea what came over him. The words were out before he realized what he'd said.

She blinked then tilted her head. "I beg your pardon? I am not certain I heard you correctly."

"You heard what I said. While I'm unable to follow through, I'm still a man with normal urges and would like to kiss you."

He pulled her toward him until he could cup her face. Her eyes widened but she made no move to stop him. She appeared mesmerized.

When their lips met, hers were soft and sweet. Her mouth parted in a soft sigh and he deepened the kiss. He would have kept her near but she pulled away to stand.

"She touched her lips. "What have I done? This is forbidden between us. You are my patient." She turned and hurried from the room.

Daniel lay there in thought. Clara was the only woman he'd seen besides family since his accident. Maybe that's why he'd not desired a particular woman before Clara came. Perhaps there was hope for him after all.

***

Clara shut her door behind her. Poor man had been so unhappy. Who would not be in his position? Rebecca teased him about being grumpy, but he probably did not think that was correct.

His kiss. She touched her fingers against her lips. Other young men had tried to kiss her—she had even let two of them. Tonight her reaction was very different.

She scolded herself for returning his kiss. When Daniel's lips touched hers, she had grown warm all over and tingles rushed down to her toes. How she had longed to nestle against his broad chest, to stretch out beside him.

Scandalous thoughts like those must be put behind her. No matter how attracted she was to him, he was her patient and she must keep their relationship professional. Never before had she let a patient become so familiar—not in that way. Some hugged her and gave her cheek a kiss when they were leaving her care.

Walking to the window, the smooth wooden floor felt cool to her feet. She peered out and saw a fox searching for prey. Would a mouse be as captivated by the fox as she had been by Daniel?

Enough fanciful thoughts. She climbed back into her bed. Hoping for a dream with more forbidden kisses, she closed her eyes.

***

The following morning, Clara took a deep breath and braced herself before she went into Daniel's room. That kiss had ruined more than her sleep. Now it would hang between them, making both self-conscious.

"Good morning, Daniel. Are you ready to have a sponge bath and face the day?"

Before he answered, she poured water from the pitcher into the basin. Carrying the basin, his soap, and a clean cloth, she set the bath things where he could reach them. Then, she got a fresh one of the cloths he used as diapers.

He's a plate and I'm washing dishes. He's a plate and I'm washing dishes.

No matter how many times she told herself otherwise, Daniel was flesh and blood and so was she, as their kiss had reminded her all too much. She would simply proceed as if nothing had happened. At least, she would try. He was so handsome and intelligent and could be funny. No wonder her mind was a jumble.

She pretended to be busy while he washed his genitals. He handed her the cloth and towel and she moved the basin out of the way to help him turn over. She was washing his back when Kathryn came in.

"I wanted to look at those two places again that tried to become bed sores."

Daniel raised his head. "Have you two forgotten I'm not a cabbage or a science experiment?"

Kathryn swatted his rear lightly. "Of course not, but don't tempt me while you're in such a vulnerable position."

Clara pointed to the places for Kathryn and spoke for his benefit, "Daniel, they have almost disappeared now that you are up so much."

Kathryn leaned near and ran a finger over them. "They'll clear completely now. Thank goodness, because bed sores are such a serious problem."

"It is amazing to me that you prevented them for two years. I am very proud to know such an accomplished healer."

Surprise shot across Kathryn's face. "Why, thank you, Clara. Well, I'll leave you and Daniel to get on with getting ready for breakfast."

After Clara had helped Daniel turn onto his back again, she washed his legs and feet. She was careful not to make eye contact when she helped him with his diaper. How humiliating this must be for a man.

"Do you wish to wear day clothes or your nightshirt?" A secretive glance proved he was avoiding looking at her.

"I'll stick with the nightshirt. Covers me down to my knees and is a lot easier than pants."

She handed him a fresh garment. "Good thing Emma has help with the laundry. We generate a lot."

"Thank you for including her with your handkerchief gifts. She's like a second mother to me. When Mama is calling on one of her patients, Emma fills in at home."

"She is protective of you and I can tell she loves you. How long has she been with your family??"

He scrunched his brow. "As near as I can remember, she came when I was three or four. Say, did you know bullfrogs don't sleep"

"I do not know where you learned that but do you not question the time someone spent on such a subject?"

"Aw, some university professor without a real job I guess."

"Being a professor *is* a job, one that Uncle Hans held. Are you ready to move to your chair?"

"Here I go, doing your work again."

***

On the first Thursday in July, Clara sat at what she'd come to think of as her place. She marveled at the quantities of food served in this house. Today's breakfast looked to be no different. Good thing she worked so hard or she'd gain weight.

After the blessing, Kathryn clapped her hands. "Time to make plans for Saturday's celebration."

Clara spread her napkin across her lap. "If I may ask, what celebration is this?"

Austin set down his cup. "July 4th is our Independence Day, the day we celebrate our 1776 Declaration of Independence from British rule. There's a picnic in the park with games and fireworks."

"Like Bastille Day in France?"

A frown creased Austin's brow. "Didn't know about Bastille Day. Probably most countries have some sort of national festival."

"How long does this celebration last?"

Her host appeared to ponder for a few seconds. "We get to the park about three in the afternoon but some folks arrive around ten and stay all day. This is a chance to see friends we don't see often. Every family brings food to contribute and the meal is served about six."

He smiled at his wife. "Kathryn's food disappears first because everyone knows she's such a good cook."

Rebecca said, "I'm not entering them this year, but there are games like a three-legged race, balancing an egg on a spoon, tug of war, and others."

Kathryn leaned forward and peered at her son. "Daniel, do want to stay here or go?"

He crossed his arms over his chest. "I'm staying here. Clara should go. I can use a day off."

Clara looked from him to his mother. "Of course, I will remain here. Daniel should not be alone for so many hours."

Emma rose to refill coffee cups. "I'll stay here with Daniel. Being out in the heat is not my idea of fun. We'll have our own celebration with his favorite foods." She winked at Daniel. "I might even let him beat me at checkers."

Kathryn smiled at the housekeeper. "That's nice of you, Emma. Seeing how we honor Independence Day should be interesting to Clara."

Rebecca raised her arms. "Yay! Clara, if you want me to I'll take you around and introduce you to people."

Clara's stomach jumped to her throat. Here in the McClintock home, she felt secure and welcome—except for Daniel's stubbornness. Was she ready to meet so many others? What if they reacted like his grandmother?

"I-If you are certain, then I will be honored to go with you. What may I do to help prepare the things you take with you?"

Emma set down the coffee pot then patted Clara's shoulder. "Choose the coolest dress you own. After all these years, Kathryn and I have a system. Rebecca helps, too. You just take care of our boy until time to leave the house."

Chapter Eight

Saturday afternoon, Clara donned the coolest dress she owned. The blue dotted Swiss trimmed in white lace had a white dimity inset at the front in tiny tucks. She loved the dress and had been told it flattered her complexion and her eyes.

After she removed the green ribbon from her straw bonnet, she replaced it with one the same shade as her dress. The hat's white flowers went with any ensemble. She hoped the McClintock family would find her appearance acceptable.

She was ready when Daniel banged on their adjoining wall. After grabbing her purse, she hurried to see what he needed.

He held a sheet of paper. "I made a family chart so you can keep everyone straight. You'll meet so many family and almost-family that they'll become a blur. Hard to keep everyone's relationship straight."

She accepted the paper and scanned the sheet. "Thank you. My goodness, what a lot of names. You are correct, today will be confusing."

"Don't worry. You'll be fine as long as you don't eat any of Avis Dunhill's cooking."

"I do not know this woman."

"When you get to the park, you'll see long tables set up to hold the food. As people arrive or when it's near time to eat, they put the dishes they brought on the tables. I tried some of her cake once and thought I'd eaten sand."

Clara chuckled. "Certainly, I will avoid her food if I can. Thank you for this guide. Good bye."

When they were on their way, the wagon was filled with quilts, baskets of food, and containers of water. She was not certain what some bundles contained. On her journey with Dr. Sullivan, she'd been too upset to pay attention. This time on the drive, she was able to enjoy the scenery.

Rebecca pointed to a lovely house. "That's where the Claytons live. Josh is married to their daughter Nettie and their son Lance used to help Daniel."

Clara referred to her paper guide. "Yes, I see."

Rebecca leaned closer. "What is that in your hand?"

"Daniel created this chart showing who is related to whom and how. He said otherwise I would not be able to keep people straight."

Kathryn turned from the front bench where she sat with Austin. "What a good idea. I wish I'd thought of that."

They arrived at the park and there were families and couples already with their blankets spread. Band music drifted across from the gazebo on which hung red, white, and blue bunting. In a shady area among a group of trees, long tables were covered with tablecloths and what appeared to be bed sheets. Food, covered by cup towels, spread across the tables.

Austin pulled near the tables. "You ladies wait here while I unload the food."

Kathryn pointed at the baskets. "The one with the red checked cloth is fried chicken. The one with the blue checked cover is desserts. Those other two go with the vegetables. The largest one nearest me is for our blanket."

He sent her a tolerant smile. "I know, I know, Sweetheart. Same every year."

She leaned back against the wagon bench. "I guess I worry too much."

Rebecca gestured to a huge tree. "Mama, I see our favorite spot. I'm going to make sure no one else takes it."

She climbed down from the wagon and took the top quilt from the stack. She reached the tree ahead of another group who'd headed that way. Rebecca pretended not to see them and spread the quilt.

Clara leaned toward Kathryn. "What was I thinking? Should I have gone with her and spread another of the covers?"

"When people see her they'll remember we need a lot of space for our family. And, we have the drinks, dishes, more quilts, and chairs for Gran and Grandpa. Let's wait and let Austin drop us off closer."

Clara relaxed. "Do the men who work for you attend?"

"Yes, this is one reason why I prepare so much food. Traditionally bachelors don't bring food. To be sure, I've told them they don't need to bring anything but their appetites."

"That is nice of you and I'm sure they are grateful for your thoughtfulness."

"We have good men working for us and we want them to know we appreciate them. I prepare extra, too, for those who can't afford to bring much."

Austin returned to drive them close to their chosen spot. When everything was unloaded, he moved the wagon near others and took care of the horses before joining them.

Rebecca helped spread the other quilts then disappeared and returned with a young woman who looked to be her age. The girls were a contrast. Rebecca had blond hair and wore a pink dress while her friend had dark brown hair and wore red checks. "This is my best friend, Maddie. We're going to go watch the games, Clara. Do you want to join us?"

Clara was torn. "Do you mind if I just sit in the shade and relax? I love watching people from this comfortable spot."

"Of course not. Join us if you change your mind." Rebecca left, chatting with her friend.

Only a slight breeze blew, but the shade of a huge tree offered respite from the sun. The quilt was soft and Clara's tensions sifted from her body.

She looked up when Kathryn sighed. "You must be very tired after preparing all this food." She couldn't imagine any family having such resources.

Kathryn removed her bonnet. "Now I can relax, though. Bless her, Emma started cooking cakes and pies yesterday. Plus, she boiled eggs and did everything possible to make this morning easier."

Clara studied the paper from Daniel. "You have a large family. How nice to have everyone living so near."

"Wonderful. I would hate for any one of my children to move far away. I want to see them often and to play with my grandchildren."

"And, now you have a lovely grandson as well as Dallas' two."

Kathryn glowed at the mention of her grandchildren. "This will be the first July 4th celebration Josh has missed. Nettie has attended two of them."

Two smiling strangers approached, the man carrying an infant.

Kathryn whispered Finn and Stella O'Neill and her father Council Clayton. Clara located them on the paper.

Kathryn waved. "Stella, Finn, Council, this is Clara Van Hoosan." She leaned near. "Their baby is Vincent Dallas O'Neill, who is six months old and one of those I delivered."

Clara nodded. "Pleased to meet you." Finn was shorter than the McClintock men but very nice looking. His lovely wife's gorgeous red hair hung free. Council was of medium height with brown hair.

Kathryn gestured toward the newcomers. "Council is the local barber. Finn and Stella partner with Dallas in breeding horses. Folks, Clara is here to help Daniel."

Stella sat on the blanket and took her baby from Finn. "I think everyone in town knows why you're here, Clara. We're happy you've come and are so hopeful for Daniel."

Council nodded. "My daughter's right. The whole town is buzzing about the miracle worker who's come. My wife will be sorry to have missed you, but she's staying with our daughter, Nettie, and helping with the new baby." Like his daughter Stella, he spoke with an English accent.

Within an hour, they had been joined by Dallas and Cenora and their two children, the rest of the O'Neill family, the McDonalds, and Grandpa and Gran.

Grandpa settled in his chair and chuckled. "This is a feast of kin, isn't it?"

Gran straightened the folds of her skirt and muttered under her breath before saying, "Half the people in the county are under this tree."

Austin appeared apologetic. "Gran, would you like some lemonade?" How sad a fine man like Austin had to be nervous about what his mother would say.

"Not yet, Son. Clara, is that right? Thank you again for the fine handkerchiefs."

"My pleasure, Mrs. McClintock. You are looking lovely today."

Gran preened. "While you're here helping Daniel, you should call me Gran."

"Thank you, Gran. I appreciate your allowing me to do so."

Family members looked at one another as if they couldn't believe what they were hearing. She could almost hear their thoughts—had Gran undergone some miraculous change?"

Gran proved not when she turned her attention to Mac O'Neill's young wife. "Vourneen, don't tell me you have another on the way so soon."

Vourneen O'Neill giggled nervously and spoke with an Irish brogue. "I won't tell you then but sure and Sean and Peggy are going to have a brother or sister in September."

Her husband, Mac, glared at Gran. "Children are a blessing from God 'tis true."

Gran peered down her nose. "Harrumph, you're going to be blessed into the poorhouse if you keep up this rate."

Vourneen's father, Colin McDonald, looked ready to jump to his daughter and son-in-law's defense.

Austin quickly said, "You've heard about Nettie and Josh's baby boy, haven't you? Everyone's doing fine except we like to have lost Josh."

The tension broke and everyone laughed.

Kathryn widened her eyes at Gran then turned to Cenora's mother. "Aoiffe, are you keeping well?"

"Since you cured me years ago, I'm fit as a fiddle and enjoying my sweet home that Dallas gave us. Sure and 'tis such a pleasure to live there."

Clara wondered what Aoiffe's illness had been. In spite of declaring herself well, she looked fragile, unlike her daughter. Cenora was a beautiful woman with auburn hair darker than that of her mother and, apparently, with boundless energy. She laughed at toddler Houston's antics while caring for baby Kate, sent loving glances at Dallas, and still participated in conversation with those around her.

Aoiffe's rounded husband, Brendan O'Neill, slapped a hand on his thigh. "Aye, and don't we have a grand garden this year with plenty o' vegetables to share? We've kept some, sold some, and given some away. Never would I have believed a poor Irishman such as meself would have such luck."

Austin laughed. "The luck of the Irish, right?"

The others—except Gran—joined in. Gran at least smiled, which transformed her face. She must have been a beautiful woman when younger. If she smiled more she would still be quite attractive.

Clara was relieved when it was time to eat.

Kathryn issued plates and eating utensils to everyone who'd come with her. She served Gran and Grandpa from the large hamper on the quilt.

"You will return to me each of the things you've taken. First, perhaps Brendan will give us a blessing."

He rose to his feet, his face beaming. "Weel, now, I know just the one." He cleared his throat and puffed out his chest. "May the road rise to meet you, may the wind be always at your back, the sun shine warm upon your face, the rain fall soft upon your fields, and until we meet again may God hold you in the hallow o' his hand. Amen."

Austin rubbed his hands together. "Thank you, Brendan. Now, let's eat."

Rebecca guided Clara to the serving tables. She pointed to one cake and whispered. "That's from Avis Dunhill. Don't get any."

"Daniel warned me. Perhaps we should take some and throw it away so the poor woman doesn't feel slighted."

"Later, right now I'm filling my plate with food I'll eat."

Clara was amazed at how much food others were piling on their pates. She understood, though, because there were so many varieties offered.

Rebecca insisted they go back for seconds. Clara took a huge slice of Mrs. Dunhill's untouched cake.

Rebecca whispered, "You can't mean to eat that?"

"No, but she will not know. Do you not think it sad that no one takes any of her cake? I would not want her feelings to be hurt."

"Okay, now I feel bad. I'll do the same." Rebecca cut a hefty portion.

When they passed a rubbish bin, both women secretly broke up the servings they'd taken of the cake and dropped the remains into the container.

Rebecca giggled. "We're only encouraging her. Next year she'll probably bring two cakes."

Before they had finished eating, Grandpa stood. "Time for speeches. Mine's short but you know Mayor Quinlan. Prepare to be bored for an hour."

The mayor stood on the gazebo and gave a long speech praising the community and all it offered. His droning on with her stomach full and a soft quilt in the shade had Clara growing sleepy until the mayor caught her attention.

"Folks, this year we're having a special ceremony. Fifty years ago, the young couple you know as Vincent and Zarelda McClintock settled here and established our town. This evening, the town council would like to present this plaque to Vincent and Zarelda McClintock for having the courage and foresight to settle here, plan our town, and invite others to join him."

Applause rippled across those gathered.

Mayor Quinlan motioned to Grandpa. "Step over here, Vincent, and say a few words." After handing over the plaque, the mayor stepped aside.

Grandpa appeared poleaxed. "Don't think I've ever been this surprised. I'm proud of this town and the people who live here. My wife and I thank you."

More applause resounded while Grandpa wended his way back to his family amid people congratulating him.

He sat in his chair and handed the plaque to Gran. "Guess I'll have to quit saying rude things about Mayor Quinlan."

Gran read the plaque. "Oh, I hate that now people will know we're old."

Austin rose and gave his mother a hug. "No one thinks you're old, Gran. But, they know you have a son who's forty-seven and, therefore, can't be in your twenties."

Gran patted his arm. "I know, but hearing the mayor announce to everyone that we've been here fifty years was a shock. I don't feel old enough to have a son your age. Actually, inside I feel about your age, Austin. Of course, not when I look in the mirror."

Grandpa chuckled and patted held his wife's hand. "My bones tell me my age anytime I try to do anything that involves moving."

Rebecca pointed to a group of men and boys. "Look, they're going to light the fireworks."

Loud bangs preceded the sky lighting with a shower of bright colors.

Happiness wrapped a veil around Clara. How nice to be among friends on a night like this. Momentarily she thought of Daniel and hoped he was being spoiled by Emma. America was a wonderful place, at least for Clara.

When she'd settled in a comfortable haze, a flare caught her eye. "Cover the children! The rocket is coming!"

She leaped into action with others. She grabbed one of the quilts and tossed it over the babies as the flares struck. Panicked people ran toward them. Rebecca and her friend led the way.

Most of the wayward sparks landed on Gran. She screamed and beat at spots on her dress with Grandpa's help. Clara picked up the older woman and rolled her in a quilt to put out the fire. When she uncovered her, the flames were extinguished but smoking.

"I'm sorry to have handled you so roughly, but I was afraid the fabric would melt to your body. Are you all right now?"

"I...I believe so. My dress is ruined and so is the nice handkerchief you gave me." She held out her hands and blisters already were forming.

Grandpa hugged Clara. "Thank you for your quick thinking and saving my wife. There were so many places we couldn't get to them all. They were erupting into flames and spreading."

Austin cradled his mother as if she were a small child. "You sure you're all right? Kathryn has her medical bag, Mama. You sit back on your chair and let her take care of you."

Gran kept her hands slightly curled and close to her body. "Your father's hands need looking after."

"That would mean yours do, too." Kathryn took one of Gran's hands. "Good heavens, you must be in pain."

Rebecca was out of breath. "Gran, I'm so sorry this happened to you."

A man with a badge rushed up to Austin. "Anyone seriously hurt?"

"My parents' hands are burned. Kathryn is tending to them. Mother's dress is ruined. What the hell happened?"

The sheriff looked ready to punch someone. "That Dexter Farris was drunk and fell against the base for the roman candles. Sent some right at you. I'll let him sober up in jail and stay there 'til he's learned a lesson."

Dallas still held his son. "With Dexter, that'll mean a life sentence."

Grandpa looked up while Kathryn treated his wounds. "Clara, Miss Van Hoosan saved my wife. The flames were spreading faster than we could beat them out. Everyone was trying to save the children, which is right of course, but they didn't notice Zarelda needed help."

The sheriff held out his hand to Clara. "Tom Yates is my name. Sure pleased to meet you." When he noticed her hands had burns, he pulled his back. "Sorry, but reckon Kathryn will tend to your burns, too. We're all hoping you can help Daniel walk again. Looks like you're a genuine miracle worker."

Stella held baby Vincent Dallas. "That's right. She threw a quilt over the children and then rushed to Gran. By the time I realized we were in danger, Clara had acted."

Clara shrugged. "I was facing the way the rocket shot from. You young mothers were not."

Kathryn finished with Gran and Grandpa. She held out her arm to Clara. "Let me see your burns. Thank you for saving the day."

Clara glanced at the quilt in which she'd wrapped Gran. "I'm afraid two of your lovely quilts have scorched and burned places on them."

"Better them than people. That silly Dexter hasn't half a brain when he's sober, which is not often." Kathryn applied soothing ointment on Clara's hands before she bandaged them.

"As soon as the ointment was on the burns, they hurt less. They feel much better. Thank you, Kathryn."

The healer closed her medical bag and stood. "I think our celebration is over and it's time to go home."

The men helped fold quilts while Kathryn collected eating utensils.

Austin laid his arm around his wife's shoulders. "I'll bring the wagon. You gonna be okay here while I do?"

She smiled at him. "Of course I will, but thank you for asking."

When they had loaded what seemed like twice what they brought, they climbed on the wagon and headed for home.

Chapter Nine

Clara stuck her head in Daniel's room to check on him before she went to bed.

The hour was late but he was still awake. He looked up from the book he'd been reading. "How did your first Independence Day Celebration go?"

"Can I tell you tomorrow? We had an eventful evening."

He shut the book and laid it aside. "Not after that teaser. Why are there bandages on your hands and burned spots on your dress?" He patted the bed beside him.

She ventured closer but stood. "The afternoon was lovely. Thank you for that chart or I would never have kept people straight. Not certain I have everyone's name memorized even with your help. I remember the English are the Claytons and that the O'Neills and McDonalds are Irish."

Changing her mind, she sat at the foot of his bed. "Your grandparents received a grand plaque commemorating the fact they founded the town fifty years ago. The mayor presented the award."

"No kidding?"

"Your grandfather said he will not make rude comments about Mayor Quinlan after this."

Daniel reared back his head and laughed. "Sure he will. They've been friendly adversaries for as long as I can remember. What else happened?"

"A man named… Dexter something… never mind, he was drunk and somehow sent some rockets into the crowd. The crowd specifically being your family. Gran's dress caught on fire but she's all right. Kathryn took care of the burns on hers and Grandpa's hands."

Daniel held up a hand. "Wait, let me get this straight. Gran let Mama doctor her?"

"Yes, fortunately your mother had her medical bag with her. Both Gran and Grandpa had burns." She held up her hands to display her own bandages.

"Clara, you don't understand the importance of the occasion. In all the time my parents have been married, Gran has never, and I mean *never*, as in *not once*, let Mama give her medical advice or take care of her. Not even a cup of herbal tea. Nothing."

"Really? How odd when your mother is so good."

"We know that and Gran probably has all along, but she refused to let Mama near her and has criticized her healing every time she saw Mama."

"Something must have happened. Perhaps having her dress on fire changed her." She tilted her head in thought. "No, before that happened, she told me to call her Gran and thanked me for the handkerchiefs."

"Amazing! Has to be one of the mysteries of the universe."

"Did Emma sufficiently spoil you in our absence?"

"In my opinion spoiling me too much is impossible. In answer, she did pamper me." He patted his abdomen. "I couldn't eat another bite. Plus, I beat her at checkers three out of five games."

At once the night's drama took toll and she thought she must lie down immediately or fall. "The hour is late and I must go to sleep. Good night, Daniel."

"G'night."

***

The next morning, Clara removed the bandages from her hands, pleased to see the burns had scabbed over. She wondered about Grandpa and Gran's injuries, which were much more serious.

At breakfast, Daniel spilled coffee on himself. "Damn. Look what I've done. How the hell could I be so clumsy?"

Kathryn snapped, "Watch your language, young man. As for spilling, everyone has an accident occasionally."

He held his nightshirt away from his body. "Sorry, Mama, but that coffee was hot."

Clara noticed he had finished his breakfast and so had she. "Let us go to your room and wash off the coffee and find you something clean, shall we?"

In his room, she searched through his folded clothing in the chest. Her fingers touched a volume and she pulled it out to examine.

She was surprised when she opened the book and read. "A book of poetry?"

He stretched out his hand. "Hey, that's private. Either put it back or give it to me. You have no right to read my writings."

She paid no attention to his demand as she read. "Daniel, these are wonderful. Have you had any of them published?"

He used his hands to sit up. "Of course not. Close the book now, Clara. I mean it."

Shaking her head, she read one aloud.

"<u>Home</u>

Weary as I head for home,
After a long day
Of the work I love.
I revel in the feast
Of my senses.
I feel the caress
Of the spring breeze,
Hear the rustling
Of the majestic trees,
And smell the sweetness
Of the lush, green grass.

As the sun sets,
The crystal blue sky
Turns to the colors
Of the sunset.
In rich hues
Of purple, orange,
And precious gold.
This is my home,
And my heart
Is full."

When she'd finished, she closed the book and sighed. "You are gifted at many things. You paint, keep records, and write poetry."

"I keep Pa's records and I'm good at that. I dabble at oil painting and water colors. My poems are stupid and private."

His self-abasement angered her. "Don't be selfish with your talent. God gave you abilities to be used. Does not the Bible say you must not hide your light under a basket?"

He threw up his hands and flopped back on the pillows. "Why do I even try to argue with you? You always turn an argument against me."

She set the book on top of the chest and gathered up a clean nightshirt. She tossed it to his bed then grabbed a washcloth and towel and poured water into a basin.

He pulled the soiled shirt over his head and dropped it onto the floor before laying against his pillows once more.

Clara sat on the bed and wrung out the cloth. Without thinking she washed his chest and rib cage where the coffee had spilled. She became aware of his heated gaze and satisfied smile.

She handed him the cloth. "I think you are enjoying this far too much. Clean yourself."

He laughed and dried his torso. "I believe you did a very nice job. Too bad you stopped." He pulled the clean garment over his head.

She took the basin to empty and the pitcher to refill. When she returned, he asked, "Did you know that all the swans in England belong to Queen Victoria?"

Astonished at his need to throw these random facts at her, she sat down the pitcher and basin. "Where do you get these tidbits?"

"Just want you to know you aren't the only educated person in the room."

She set down the pitcher and basin. "Well, did you know that no piece of paper can be folded in half more than seven times?"

He frowned. "What? I don't believe you. Give me a sheet of paper. There's some in the bedside table."

She handed him a piece of the white paper. "That should keep you busy for a while. I'll put this soiled nightshirt in the laundry hamper." That task done, she picked up his poetry journal and read it aloud while he worked.

"*As Life Continues*

At First,
The world stopped.
Everything in our lives
Was The Accident.
Friends, family, doctors,
All keeping vigil
With love and support.
Quiet murmurs
That everything would be
Good again soon.
But time is relentless.
It moves on
Without fail.
Lives and routines resumed.
Friends returned home.
Family continued to work,
Consumed with the
Necessary tasks of life.
Yet I stay still.
Broken of body and heart.
Trapped in my new,
Useless, body.
Unable to move on
To grow and to prosper.
Life is divided
Pre and post accident.
And I remain stagnant.
Alive,
Yet not living."

    She sighed. "Daniel, that is poignant and heartbreaking. You are talented."

    He paid no attention as he folded. Then, he unfolded and started over. When the folded paper hit her, she looked at him.

    He declared, "It's only impossible because the folds become so thick. Maybe Grizzly could get more."

    "If you are admitting defeat, let us get busy on your exercises.

Your cousins will not be here today and we are free to concentrate right away."

He groaned. "Slave driver."

Their banter was interrupted when Gran appeared. "I came to have my bandages changed and thought I'd watch your exercises." She stared at the bars. "This is rather impressive. Clara, did you set this up alone?"

"I did. I brought the materials from Amsterdam. Daniel and I use them each day. During weekdays, Josh and Dallas come to give Daniel walking lessons. I'm sorry they won't be here today to show you how clever they are."

Gran gave a flick of her hand. "Austin described their method. He also mentioned that you can now move your toes, Daniel, so I suppose you are making progress."

"Clara insists. I was telling her she's a slave driver when you came in."

"So I heard. Well, let's see some action."

Under Gran's scrutiny, Clara hooked the harness onto Daniel and made certain his hands were secure on the parallel bars. She squatted in front of him and duck-walked backwards while moving his feet. As always, at the end of the bars, she helped him turn. Then, preceded him toward the place where they had begun. Over and over they made the same route.

On the third trek, Gran stood. "I don't know how you can work like that, Clara. You must have very strong legs and an aching back."

"When Daniel naps, I sometimes lie down for a bit."

"I see you're no longer wearing a dressing on your hands. I hope that means you weren't badly burned."

"I am fine. I hope you are not in pain."

She held up her hands, turning them this way and that to examine their bandages. "Not unless I pick up something firm. By the way, I intend to replace the dress that was ruined while helping me."

"That is not necessary. You were not responsible for the accident."

"I insist. I'll have my seamstress call on you this week. Now, I must go find my husband. Vincent and I are missing church today. I didn't feel like dressing up and facing all the questions that were certain to bombard us. Besides, we'd arranged to have the bandages changed today."

"I can understand your seeking privacy. People's curiosity can be very trying even though they mean well."

"Daniel, you keep working. I expect next time I come you'll have made even more progress. Goodbye to both of you."

Daniel called, "Gran, aren't you staying for dinner?"

She stopped in the doorway and shook her head. "Another time. Yesterday upset me and right now, I want to go home."

When Gran had gone, Daniel begged to be allowed a nap. When he was stretched out on the bed, Clara read aloud another of his poems.

"Scout
One moment,
One tiny, excruciating moment,
And your life stopped
In a cacophony of pain
And confusion.
My partner,
My companion
Breathed his last
And ceased to be.
When they told me
You were gone
I wept.
And now,
As I lay
Mired in pain,
I miss you,
Old friend."

She closed the book. "That almost made me cry."

His face grew red. "You're making fun of me."

"That was a compliment. These are beautiful, sensitive poems. I envy your ability to write. That you can also paint is unfair."

He gestured at the walls. "If there's a painting you want, take it."

"Really? You would give me one?" She laid the poetry journal on the chest of drawers.

He shrugged but didn't meet her eyes. "It's not a big deal if you want to choose one. Don't feel obligated, though."

"Each painting is wonderful." Slowly, she walked the length of his room and gazed at the pictures and stopped in front of her favorite. "I especially love the one of this home. I had planned to ask Rebecca how much they sell for and see if I could afford this."

He burrowed into his pillows. "If you'll let me sleep for an hour, it's yours."

"You have a deal." She took the painting from the wall and left his room before His Orneriness changed his mind.

***

Two days later during Daniel's rest time, unusual guests arrived. Kathryn answered the door then called Clara from her room.

A beautifully dressed woman of middle age paused in the middle of the parlor and clapped her hands shoulder height. "I am Madame Thibodaux and this is my assistant, Sylvie. I have come to measure a dress for Miss Van Hoosan." Madame's dress was black taffeta of the latest style.

Sylvie was about forty, thin, and almost haggard. Her dress was also black and very plain, though, a lovely style.

Kathryn grinned mischievously. "Clara, I don't think you need my help with these ladies."

The dressmaker stared aghast. "What is this… this terrible costume you wear?" She walked around Clara as if she were a specimen in a museum.

"My uniform. I am a mechanotherapist here to treat Daniel McClintock." Clara gestured toward her room. "We can talk in there."

"Talk? No, you must remove those horrid clothes and strip to your chemise. Quickly." She clapped her hands again.

Did this person speak this imperiously to Gran? Clara led the two women into her room then closed the door.

"Are you certain I must undress?"

"*Oui*, to your chemise." She clapped her hands again. "My tape, Sylvie."

Although Clara resented Madame's attitude, she was excited to have a new dress sewn by a dressmaker. She undressed and stood for Madame to measure her.

"What is this? You wear no corset? Scandalous."

"I need freedom of movement for my work."

Madame measured and tut tutted and called numbers to her assistant.

Clara asked, "Is something wrong, Madame Thibodaux?"

The woman snapped, "Do not move while I am working. If one overlooks the fact that you do not wear a corset, then nothing is amiss. The fabric Mrs. Vincent McClintock chose for you will be lovely with your complexion and hair."

"What kind and color of fabric?"

"Silk and faille in blue the color of your eyes and trimmed in Honiton lace. You know Queen Victoria's wedding costume was of this same lace. This dream creation I will construct especially for you in the latest fashion. You will look lovely and, of course, the dress will be magnificent."

Clara had to suppress laughter at the dressmaker's conceit. "When will it be ready?"

Madame waved dismissively. "It will be ready when it is ready. Do not concern yourself. I will bring the garment here for a fitting. You have to do nothing." She clapped her hands at Sylvie, who hurried to take charge of the tape measure.

"Have you finished with me for today?"

"Yes. I suppose you plan to put on that horrid costume again." She shuddered. "It is unflattering and ugly. Why do you wear it?"

"I explained that I am a mechanotherapist. I must wear clothing that allows me to get on the floor, to give a massage, and to move in various ways while I work with my patient. I can't be hindered by a corset, wide skirts, or lots of petticoats and ruffles."

Madame tut tutted again. "This color is not good for you. You should have this in gray if you want it to look like a uniform. Yes, a blue-based gray would be much better."

Clara was surprised she liked Madame's idea. "When I sew a new one, I will choose gray."

"Good. We will be back to fit the dress. *Bonne après midi.*"

"*Bonne après-midi. Merci d'être venu. J'ai hâte de voir la robe.*"

Madame's eyes rounded. "Come, Sylvie." The two left in a rush.

As soon as they had gone, Kathryn sauntered into the room.

"What did you think of the local modiste?"

"I didn't have time to think much, except that she is as French as we are."

Kathryn laughed. "You're clever. I didn't understand what you said, but I heard you speak what I think was French to her. I'll bet she was surprised."

"I only bid her good afternoon and thanked her for coming and told her I look forward to seeing the dress. She rushed away right after that."

Kathryn was still laughing. "Her real name is Bertha Wellburn, but she's from San Antonio, not France as she pretends."

Clara laughed too. "I suppose she thinks a French dressmaker will be more in demand."

"She's right and she's very good. Poor Sylvie must lead a harried life. Madame treats the woman like a slave. In some way they're related but I don't remember how."

"I told Gran there was no need for her to replace my dress. I have figured a way to cut out the burned section and use the panniers as replacement fabric. I think no one will know the difference."

Kathryn raised her eyebrows. "When Gran makes up her mind to do something, it's best to go along."

Clara giggled. "I must admit I am excited to have a new dress neither my aunt nor I sewed."

When she went back to Daniel's room, he was reading.

He closed the book. "That sounded like quite an experience. So, you speak French."

"Most people in The Netherlands speak at least smatterings of French and English and German and Danish plus some Dutch dialects. America is so large you do not realize how small the countries are in that part of Europe. People travel back and forth easily."

"Do you speak all those languages?"

"Yes. To be in business, one needs them. If I had remained in my little village with my parents, I doubt I would know more than a few Dutch dialects."

"Hmm, I manage a little—very little—Texas German. Many Germans settled in this part of Texas in the last century. I speak Spanish very well, at least the Texas version, which is more Mexico than Spain.

You need to learn. You're bound to have Mexican patients who don't speak much English."

"That is a good idea. Perhaps you can teach me—if you will not trick me so I say rude things without knowing I am."

He grinned and laid his right hand on his heart. "I can teach you and I won't deceive you, I promise. Since you know so many languages, you'll pick up a new one in no time."

"This has been a good day. I am getting a new dress and have found a language teacher."

Chapter Ten

Two days later, Madame Thibodaux and Sylvie showed up. Fortunately, once again they arrived during Daniel's rest time. They went immediately to Clara's room. Madame carefully unwrapped and revealed the dress.

Clara was dumbstruck.

Madame snapped, "Well, what do you think? Have you no words today?"

Clara clasped her hands to her chest. "This is the most beautiful dress I've ever seen."

Madame preened. "But of course. Did I not say it would be magnificent? Off with that distressing uniform so I can judge how this fits."

Eager to try the gown, Clara hurriedly stripped to her chemise.

The dressmaker motioned with her hands. "You will step into the dress which Sylvie will fasten for you."

Clara couldn't see the mirror from where she stood. As soon as Sylvie completed the buttons, Clara moved so she could see her reflection.

She turned from side to side and faced the mirror. "I-I am a different person. You are truly a gifted artist, Madame."

Madame made a bored expression. "Of course, but you must do something more… clever with your hair. Before you wore a long braid and now a bun. What are you thinking?"

"I am thinking of keeping my hair out of the way while I work."

"Tut tut, a woman as beautiful as you should not be working. Do you not have a man?"

Insulting as Madame was, Clara laughed. "I will never depend on a man to provide for me. If I marry, it will be because I am in love and loved."

"Too bad because that rarely happens."

"My hosts, Mr. and Mrs. Austin McClintock, are in love and so are their oldest son and his wife and their adopted son and his wife. Mr. and Mrs. Vincent McClintock also are in love. Do you find these four couples so rare?"

She placed a hand at her throat. "You have shocked me. I will have to meditate on this. Your dress will be even more magnificent when completed. I will bring it to you in a few days."

Sylvie had rewrapped the protective muslin around the gown and followed Madame from Clara's room. This time, Madame did not bid Clara farewell in French.

***

One Sunday, when everyone else had gone to church, Clara was giving Daniel his massage. She worked with each of his legs, encouraging blood flow to the muscles. His current condition troubled her.

Too much time had passed since his toes first moved. He should have had a new result by now. He was becoming negative again and she did not know how to cheer him.

"Clara?" When she looked up, he wore an odd expression.

She paused. "What is it? Are you in pain?"

"I had an odd sensation, as if my bladder was full." He tugged at his wet diaper and exposed his erect penis. "Yahoo! I work. Do you see that? I'm back a man again."

She moved beside the bed. "You were always a man. I am pleased for you that you have achieved an erection. This relieves your mind, does it not?" She turned to get a clean diaper, giving thanks that his progress would restore his will to follow her exercises.

Before she could move away, he grabbed her and pulled her beside him. "Let's make love."

She tried to pull away. "How like a man. Five minutes you have recovered your manhood and you want to have intimate relations. This is not only premature, but it is not going to happen."

He embraced her. "All right, but stay here beside me for a while. Remind me I'm still a man."

His kiss took her by surprise but she could not summon the will to force herself away. The kiss deepened and grew fervent. His hands moved over her, cupping her breasts.

She pulled away and grabbed his hand. "Stop, Daniel. You have not seen a woman who was not a family member for two years. I don't want to be your guinea pig simply because I am at hand."

He caressed her face. "You aren't a substitute, Clara. I'm crazy about you."

She leaned on her elbow in order to look into his eyes. "You do not even like me. You have told me so many times."

"You know that was frustration. I apologize if I offended you. I admire you a great deal but you intimidate me."

Her mouth dropped open. "Why would that be?"

"Because you've been halfway across the world. You've attended a university, speak all those languages, know about healing broken bodies, and are really smart."

"You are intelligent as well as gifted at painting and poetry and keeping books. Besides, you said I am a Viking."

He tucked a stray curl behind her ear. "But, that's not a bad thing. You're gorgeous, like a Viking goddess. A golden goddess with deep blue eyes. But, if I learn to walk, I'll be taller than you."

"*When* you learn to walk, you will be." She scooted so their heads were even. "Your feet are below mine several inches. But, you have on not enough clothing."

He hugged her again then released her. "I know. I wanted to celebrate with you. If you are afraid I'll break, then I'll try to convince you another time."

She would have preferred remaining beside him for a long time. Instead, she rose to get him a clean diaper. Lying there with his genitals exposed was hardly appropriate, even though she saw his body as part of her work. At least, she tried to do so. Keeping impersonal was becoming more and more difficult.

"I am supposed to remain professional and businesslike with you. I have failed at that part of my job."

"I hope that means you are at least a little attracted to me because I am very much so to you."

When he was cleaned and clothed, she sat at the foot of his bed. "Daniel, you know it is very common for a patient to think he is in love with the therapist who helps him. How long since you've seen a woman not related to you other than Emma?"

"A couple of years, but that doesn't matter. I know what I feel and it's not some crush. I've had those and I know the difference." He punched the bed with his fist. "Hell, guess it's not important because you deserve a fitter man. Besides, you said you plan to have your own clinic and I suppose that means a large city."

She shook a forefinger at him. "You are robust enough for any woman, Daniel McClintock. I do not want you to feel otherwise. Whether a man walks is *not* what makes him a man. Your mind and your heart are what make you the person I… admire."

She had almost said love. Thank goodness she had not slipped.

He met her gaze. "Do you think you could ever come to more than admire me as I do you? You said you won't lie to me."

Clara could not pretend otherwise. "Then I will admit I am growing quite fond of you. But, it is wrong of me, very wrong. Once you are walking, you will see many women and find one who suits you far better than I do. A Texas woman with whom you have many things in common will be perfect for you."

"No, you are wrong, Clara. I am falling in love with you."

She longed to crawl back beside him and lay her head on his chest. Having his arms around her had been wonderful, as if she had found home.

"Let us postpone such talk until you are walking. Then you can decide how you feel about me and other women."

"If you wish, but I know the answer now."

She rose. "Why do you not have a nap until your family returns? Perhaps I will write a letter to my aunt."

"Weren't you supposed to get a letter from your uncle's solicitor? Shouldn't it have come by now?"

"I imagine estate paperwork is rather slow."

His eyes lit with mischief. "The solicitor's probably trying to fold the papers more than seven times and that's what's taking so long."

She laughed. "You are crazy. Rest now." She fled to her room.

***

Daniel was unable to fall asleep. Clara doubted his affection, but he knew his own mind. How could he prove himself to her?

He relaxed against the pillows. At least he could now sense when he needed to pee and could do something about it. For two years he'd worried about his future with a body that deserted him.

He'd heard Grandpa tell Pa that old age was when your plumbing became more important than sex. Not true for him. Both were important, one a part of the other in him being whole. Perhaps he wouldn't have to wear a blasted diaper much longer.

Did this erection mean he could father a child? Clara didn't know the answer to that one. He wanted children, maybe three or four. He visualized the girls with blond hair like Clara's and boys with dark hair like his.

He heard her pacing next door. She'd looked aghast when he suggested they make love. He'd be willing to bet she was thinking of doing just that now.

With a smile on his lips, he drifted to sleep.

***

Clara walked back and forth in her room. Finally, she stopped and peered out the windows. The landscape was so different from that she was accustomed to in Amsterdam.

Texas, or what she'd seen of it, had a beauty all its own. She enjoyed living in this house with this family. Face it, she especially enjoyed Daniel. Not only was he handsome, he was talented and funny and smart.

Dear God, give me the skills I need to insure he walks again. If it is Your will, use me as an instrument to heal him.

What would she do if he did love her when he was healed? What a hard choice. People needed her skill, but she needed personal happiness as well. Silly woman, you know he will change his mind when he's walking.

She picked up a book and tried to read but couldn't concentrate. She tried to nap but couldn't fall asleep. She gave up and went to the kitchen to set the table and see if there was anything she could do to help prepare lunch.

By the time the family and Emma returned from church, Clara had finished the meal Emma had started early that morning.

Emma hugged her. "This is a pleasant surprise."

Kathryn and Rebecca had removed their bonnets when they entered the kitchen. Kathryn grabbed an apron then stopped. "Why, everything is ready to serve. Thank you, Clara."

Austin loosened his tie. "How long until we eat? I'm hungry as a bear coming out of hibernation."

Clara whispered in his ear. "Daniel has something important to tell you."

Frowning, Austin left the room. In spite of the other three women giving her a puzzled look, she said nothing.

Austin's loud guffaw was followed by his and Daniel's voices, though the words were indistinguishable. When he returned, Austin was pushing Daniel in the wheelchair. His smile was wide and he winked at Clara before taking his place at the table.

When everyone was seated, he bent his head. "Dear Lord, we are grateful for this food and the hands that prepared it. Use it to nourish our bodies and our minds. Thank you for sending Clara to us. Lord, we are especially grateful for the healing You have shown to our son Daniel, named after Your servant who withstood the lion's den. We thank you and ask that his healing continue. We bless Your holy name. Amen."

Kathryn looked from her husband to her son. "Well… are you going to share whatever this secret is with the rest of us?"

Austin shook his head. "Honey, some things a man can't discuss with his mother and sister, especially not at the dinner table."

Daniel just smiled and concentrated on his food.

During the meal, Clara's thoughts kept going back to the blessing. She hadn't heard her name mentioned in a blessing since the first meal she shared with Uncle Hans and Aunt Petra. In addition to her becoming more and more attracted to Daniel, she loved the McClintock family.

Leaving them would be the most difficult thing she'd ever done. Daniel was making progress and would soon be walking. She'd have no reason to remain then.

***

Late Monday, the rattle of wheels sent Clara to the window. A wagon pulled up in front of the house. The driver climbed out and went around to help a woman alight.

Clara gasped in horror then raced from the room. "My aunt has arrived. Please, don't invite her to stay. I have no idea why she would leave Amsterdam to come here."

Kathryn rose from her chair in the parlor and patted Clara's shoulder. "Calm yourself. Let's get her inside. I'm sure she's tired and likely hungry."

Austin went to the foyer and opened the door.

Aunt Petra's shrill voice and thick accent pierced Clara's ears. "Miss Clara Van Hoosan is here, ja?"

Austin held the door wide. "She is. Won't you come in? Hello, Fred. How are things at the livery?"

"This lady hired me to bring her things here. Hope it's all right."

"Of course. Let me give you a hand. Line those trunks up on the porch next to the house."

While Austin helped this Fred person unload trunks, Aunt Petra came into the parlor. "Clara, I have found you at last." She held out her arms. "Are you not happy to see me?"

Clara gave her aunt a perfunctory hug then stepped back. "Aunt Petra, why are you here?"

Her aunt stared as if Clara were addle-brained. "I told you in my letter that I was coming."

Clawing her way up from desperation's fog, Clara tried to make sense of her aunt's presence. "The letter telling me Uncle Hans had passed away did not mention you planned a trip here. You only mentioned you were lonely."

Petra held her hands palm up. "Ja, and of course I would come to you, my only relative and who is like my daughter. Surely you understood my intention."

"No, I did not." Clara had not intended her voice to sound so terse. She took a deep breath and fought to be civil. "Let me introduce my hosts. Kathryn and Austin McClintock own this ranch. This is their daughter Rebecca. And, this is Emma Harper, treasured housekeeper and cook. Friends, this is my aunt, Petra Jaager, from Amsterdam."

Kathryn smiled graciously, as she did everything. "Welcome to Texas. Won't you sit down."

Petra scanned the room. "And your patient? The boy who is paralyzed?"

"Daniel, is resting in his room."

Petra removed her hat and gloves and laid them on a table. "I am happy to meet each of you. Clara wrote to tell me how nice you are to her and how much she enjoys being here. I decided to move to McClintock Falls while Clara is here."

Clara's head was spinning. "M-Move here? What about your

home in Amsterdam?"

Petra sat on the couch and folded her hands in her lap. "I sold it." She took a deep breath. "The Van der Meers next door wanted our house to combine with theirs. Their son wants to bring his wife and two children to live with them. They need more room and made me a more than fair offer."

While Clara tried to take in Petra's explanation, Emma asked, "Have you had supper?"

Petra shook her head. "No, but I do not wish to make trouble for anyone."

Emma rose from her chair. "No trouble, I'll fix you a plate. Would you like to come to the kitchen or shall I bring the meal in here?"

Petra stood. "I will come there. Clara, are you coming with me?"

Clara summoned a smile, though she felt far from happy. "Go with Emma and I'll be there in just a moment." As soon as Emma and Petra were out of hearing, Clara hurried to Kathryn. "I am so embarrassed. I had no idea she was coming here."

Kathryn took Clara's hand. "Don't fret. You read me her letter and it gave no clue to her intentions. But, she's here and must have a place to sleep until she can find somewhere to live."

"She will share my room. The more comfortable you make her, the harder it will be to get her out of your home. Oh, I know she is lonely, but she is not a nice person."

Austin smiled at Clara. "Don't make too much of her arrival. We can find her a nice little house in town so she can walk to the store and to church if that's what you wish."

Clara sighed with relief. "Yes, thank you, that would be ideal. Perhaps she could also make friends in town and visit with other women there. I resent the way she treated me but she is my only aunt and I do not want her to be lonely."

Kathryn hugged Clara's shoulders. "Go to the kitchen. You and she can discuss what's to be done. We'll give you privacy while she eats."

"You are wonderful people. Thank you." Clara hurried to the kitchen.

Emma set a plate heaped with leftovers in front of Petra.

Searching for a topic of conversation, Clara sat across from her aunt. "Did you have difficulty on your journey?"

"The ship was tedious and I suffered from nausea. I enjoyed the train journey. I had no idea America was so large and diverse."

"There are many miles more west to the Pacific Ocean from here. The town where you got off the train is lovely and is named after Austin's father."

Petra's eyes widened and she stopped eating. "You call him by his first name? Surely not to his face?"

"He and Kathryn asked me to call them by their first names. Working here is like being a part of their family. Here in Texas, customs are not so formal. But, Petra, you will have to share my room. You are my guest, not theirs."

Petra appeared disappointed but then nodded. "This is right. If you plan to remain here after your patient is walking, then I will buy a house. If you plan to move on, then I will only rent one. That is, if there is anything available."

"I'm sure you can find something suitable. Austin said he would help you find a place located so you could walk to shops and church. His father owns many properties. Perhaps he has something suitable."

"You lived with Hans and me longer than with your parents. I believe that gives me the right to claim you as my daughter too."

"But, you never treated me as your daughter." The words slipped out before she could stop them. Her aunt looked as if she had been slapped.

Petra gasped and laid a hand on her chest. "Of course I did. I taught you to sew and cook and host a social gathering."

"Not as your daughter, more as a servant."

Petra's incredulous stare faded as she turned aside. "That is the way my parents treated me. I think all daughters are trained to serve their parents."

Perhaps that was why Petra was so cold. Perhaps she had been treated with the same coldness and knew no other way to act. This was a revelation to Clara.

She reached across to squeeze her aunt's hand. "While you are here, watch how Kathryn acts toward Rebecca. There is much love and warmth between them."

Her aunt shook her head sadly. "I am not good at showing warmth or love but that does not mean I do not feel these things here."

She patted her heart. "Your mother was affectionate and always laughing and flitting from person to person and enchanting everyone. I do not know how she did this."

"I remember she was beautiful. I loved her very much, and Papa too."

"Ja, but also she was strong-willed, which is why she died and also your Papa. You must use your will for strength of purpose and not for selfish reasons, Clara. You have a great deal to offer and can make something grand of your life."

The compliment further startled Clara. "I thought you didn't want me to be a heilgymnast."

"Ja, this is true. I would prefer you to have chosen a more feminine profession such as a teacher or nurse. At least you are filling an important need. Hans said you were very good, the best he had seen."

"He was a kind man. I am grateful he helped me. Now I have my chance and can someday build my own clinic."

Petra scoffed, "*Your own clinic*? My, that is a grand dream."

Clara thought she should change the subject. "I still have not heard from the solicitor. Do you know why he would send me a letter?"

"I have his documents with me. It's about the income from selling your parents' farm and home. Hans invested the proceeds and multiplied the sum for you."

Petra began weeping and fumbled for her handkerchief. "This is what we argued about on the day he died. He wanted to use the funds as your dowry and I said we deserved some of them for raising you. Hans was adamant that all the money go to you."

This news was a shock to Clara. "Please do not feel you caused his death. You know he had a weak heart."

Petra dabbed at her eyes with her napkin. "I cannot stop from thinking this. But, we never had a... what you call it... a vacation. The trip to attend your parents' funerals and to get you is the last one we took, although he attended many professional conferences. Twelve years and he was always too busy. I thought if we had more money, perhaps he would have taken us somewhere."

"I don't think that's why you didn't travel. He was convinced he had to work each day or things would not get done properly."

"Perhaps, but he always used money as an excuse. Then, when he died, I learned that he had invested for us as well." She met Clara's eyes. "We had plenty of money all along and so did you."

Clara's heart sped up. "Aunt Petra, how much are you talking about?"

Petra shrugged. "I have the papers in one of my trunks. I will show these to you later."

Clara pushed back from the table. "I must prepare my patient for the night. Do you want to sit in the parlor for a while or go to my room?"

"I am tired from my journey. Perhaps I could go to your room now. Should I first meet your patient?"

"If you wish." Clara helped her aunt from the table. "Come with me. Emma, thank you for preparing supper for my aunt."

Petra paused and turned to Emma. "Ja, thank you for the wonderful food."

As they went through the parlor, Clara explained her aunt's wish to turn in for the night after meeting Daniel. She ushered her aunt to Daniel's room.

"Aunt Petra Jaager, this is Daniel McClintock."

Her aunt's eyes widened. "But this is a man. I thought you were helping a boy."

Daniel chuckled. "She thought so until we met. Nice to meet you, Aunt Petra."

Petra grabbed her arm. "I do not think it is proper for a woman to work with a man. Did Hans know Daniel's age before your came?"

"No, but I worked with many men as well as women and children in Amsterdam. Surely you knew this."

She pouted. "No, Hans never talked much about his work. Neither did you. All I knew was busy or not busy, hard or easy."

Petra gestured to the equipment. "Is all this part of your treatment?"

"Yes, I brought it with me from Amsterdam. The easel is where Daniel paints the wonderful pictures you see hung on the walls."

Petra scanned the room. "You have talent, young man."

"Thank you."

Clara held her aunt's hand. "Come, let me show you the room we will share until you find where you wish to live." She widened her eyes at

Daniel as she ushered her aunt out of his room.

In her room, she lit a lamp. "Ah, here is your valise. I hope it contains all you need for tonight."

Petra turned slowly in a circle. "This is your room? So large for one person. Almost double the size of the one Hans and I shared."

"Things are different here. There is more room so houses can be larger without being as expensive as a palace. You will have many adjustments. Perhaps tomorrow you can go for a long walk and see the ranch."

"The weather is very warm, is it not? How can you sleep?"

"Do not wear your nightgown. Sleep in your chemise or the heat will make you miserable. When you go into town, you can purchase a batiste or lawn gown for sleeping. As it is, there's a nice breeze tonight and we should be quite comfortable."

Petra sat on the chair and began to remove her shoes. "I suppose I will do as you say. I see there are many differences here. I will learn as well and as fast I can."

Clara wondered about her aunt's ability to be flexible to change but didn't want to discourage her efforts. "I am certain you will do so nicely. Goodnight. I will be quiet when I return in case you are asleep."

Chapter Eleven

Clara fled to Daniel's room and paused inside his door to gather her thoughts. "I am beyond surprised." She spoke low so her aunt would not hear.

Daniel sat at his easel, motioned her near, and grinned. "You have already tucked me in. Didn't give me a goodnight kiss, though, so I couldn't sleep."

"Oh, Daniel, this is not funny. She thinks she treated me like her daughter but all she did was complain. In twelve years, not one time did she give me a compliment. I have no idea what to say to her."

"Don't worry. I heard you talking to my folks. I'd been painting and was coming to meet her when you told her I was in my room. Things will work out for both of you."

"What are you painting now?" She reached to lift the cloth covering.

He grabbed her wrist and shook his head. "I never show a painting until it's finished so you'll have to wait to find out."

She cocked an eyebrow. "I suppose all artists are temperamental."

He grinned. "I only know about myself. Wouldn't say temperamental, merely protective of my work."

She held her finger and thumb to display an inch. "Just a tiny peek?"

He chuckled. "I don't think curiosity is a cat, I think it's a woman."

"Can you blame me? I know you paint wonderfully well. Naturally, I want to see your next creation."

"Just be pleased I feel like painting again. I hadn't painted for a couple of months before you came."

"But why, when you do such great work and the money goes to the church?"

He took her hand. "Reckon I was too depressed. Every day

seemed like the one before. I couldn't face my life. Now you've given me hope." He kissed her fingers.

"Daniel, I can't guarantee anything. I believe you will walk, but I can't promise that result."

"I've made improvement since you've been here. That's what keeps me going. That, and having you near."

She sighed at his sweet remark. "You are such a good man. I want so badly for you to be healed."

"Why don't you really tuck me in for the night? I'm tired after the workout you forced on me today."

She pushed his chair to the bed. "Now you get out of the chair onto the bed."

"You take your power over me seriously, don't you?" He went through the steps and moved onto the bed.

Once he was in place for the night he lay back. "Have you ever seen a monkey or baboon? I feel like one when I move using my hands."

"In the Amsterdam zoo I have seen them. Such a handsome baboon you are, too." She kissed his forehead.

"For that, lovely Clara, you have to kiss me goodnight. Not a peck but a proper kiss."

She shook her head. "There is no such thing as a proper kiss between us."

"All right then, a passionate kiss." He pulled her forward until she was in his embrace.

His kiss melted her resistance in an instant. He lifted her so she was above him. When she thought her sanity had forsaken her, she became simultaneously aware of his erection pressing against her and his hand tugging up the hem of her skirt.

She pushed his hand away and hissed, "Are you mad? My crazy aunt is next door and likely to come to your door."

He flashed a determined gaze. "You think I'd care?"

She gave him arm a light slap. "You'd better. I'd care and so would your parents and, believe me, so would my aunt." She pulled away from him and stood. "You should sleep now."

He raised his eyebrows. "Not a chance, thanks to you."

She fled from his room before she could weaken and return to his bed.

***

Daniel pondered this new situation. The presence of Clara's aunt in the next room was definitely a problem that would mean convincing her to make love was impossible. The only thing to do was encourage Pa to find the aunt a place to live away from the ranch as soon as possible.

If he was honest, he wanted the aunt moved for Clara's benefit. She was so upset her aunt had arrived. Clara was a level-headed woman and he'd never before seen her frantic. He loved her and didn't want anything to distress her.

For himself, he desperately wanted to make love to Clara. He was certain he could now if she agreed. He wasn't soiling himself any longer.

Tomorrow, he would ask her to find his old underwear. What a relief it would be to get rid of this diaper even if he couldn't walk yet. Each milestone forward encouraged him.

For a while he'd doubted Clara. Now he believed he'd walk and soon. He'd fervently prayed he would. He knew his parents did too.

For their sake, he wanted to walk well enough to end their worry. The damned accident hadn't been his fault, but he couldn't help feeling responsible for their two years of constant concern and expense. Josh and Dallas had been faithful in helping him practice walking to the detriment of their ranches. Sure he would do the same for one of them, but that didn't mean they hadn't had to neglect their work to help him.

He'd worried so much Pa had finally told him what Clara's salary was. Not much because she had room and board provided. She apparently thought it was a fair amount. He wondered what she'd earned in The Netherlands.

One important task for him was convincing her to remain with him. He realized others needed her skill but why couldn't they come here? Together he and she could think of a way to make that happen.

Hell, why couldn't he sleep? The fault was his, not Clara's. He'd taken her further than she was willing. Result was, he was stuck thinking about bedding her while she was probably fast asleep.

***

When Clara tiptoed into her room, the lamp still burned and she heard her aunt crying softly. She rushed to the bed and touched Petra's shaking shoulder.

"Aunt Petra, what is wrong?"

Her aunt startled then faced her and dabbed at her tears with a handkerchief. "I am miserable. I can tell you do not want me here but what else am I to do? I see I was foolish to come without writing you and waiting for your answer."

Good heavens, she must not let her aunt's feeling be hurt. Time to soothe her.

Clara gave Petra a hug. "You were right to come. But, I was terribly shocked to see you here when I thought you were still in your home in Amsterdam. It's true we should be together, Aunt Petra. Austin will help you find a suitable place to live in town so you can walk to shops and church."

Petra gestured around them. "Why can't I stay here? This room has plenty of space for two."

Scrabbling for an answer, Clara mentioned the first thing that came to mind, "But what would you do all day? Kathryn is an herbal healer and midwife and is busy. Emma also is busy. If you are in town, you could visit with other women or shop. I'm sure you'll make friends right away."

Petra shook her head. "You know I do not make friends easily. Hans understood me, but others think I am cold and snobbish."

Clara gasped. "Who said that to you?"

"A few days after you left and the university wives meeting was at my home, I heard three of the wives talking when they thought I was in the kitchen. Or, I even wondered if they meant for me to hear."

Clara was incensed. "You mean they insulted you in your own home? The nerve." She undressed and hung her dress in the armoire.

"But you agree because you said I was not warm and loving."

She paused as she readied for bed. "Oh, Aunt Petra, I certainly do not agree with those women. You explained why you were not more loving to me. I hope you gave those harpies the sharp side of your tongue." She donned her nightgown.

Petra twisted her handkerchief in her hands. "I pretended I had not heard but I was very hurt. When Hans died, I no longer fit in their group so I stopped associating with them. The women from church were kinder, especially when Hans passed, but I do not think they really enjoyed my company."

Clara was surprised her aunt realized others didn't like her. How sad to recognize that fact and be unable to remedy the opinions of others. Desperation must have driven her to Texas and her only relative. Clara's feelings toward her aunt had changed this evening. Now she knew what she had to do.

She patted her aunt's shoulder. "Don't worry. I'll make certain you find good friends here. I know just the person to help you. And, I will visit you each week. Now, dry your eyes and go to sleep. I remember that journey and I know you must be exhausted."

"Ja, but I was too worried to rest." She grabbed Clara's hand. "I am glad you do not plan to send me away from here. I-I think I will like this place."

Clara squeezed her aunt's hand. "I'm sure you will. In the morning, I must rise early to get Daniel ready for breakfast. You can sleep a half hour later and still have time to join everyone in the kitchen. I'll be as quiet as I can when I rise. Goodnight, Dear Aunt." She lowered the lamp's wick.

Her aunt's heavy sigh came as a final sob. "Thank you, Clara. Goodnight."

Guilt thrashed Clara. All this time she had misunderstood her aunt. Otherwise, they might have had a close relationship. What a tragedy for both of them.

***

Two days later, Austin took Petra and Clara to town. Rebecca came with them. Their first stop was at Gran and Grandpa's.

When they were in the parlor, Clara introduced her aunt. "Gran and Grandpa, may I introduce my aunt, Petra Jaager? She was recently widowed and came to live near me because we are each other's only kin. She raised me after my parents died when I was ten." She turned to her aunt. "Aunt Petra, this is Mr. and Mrs. Vincent McClintock, Austin's parents. They founded the town."

After they exchanged greetings, they sat down and visited a few minutes before Austin slapped his knee, as if he'd sat through enough chit chat. "Petra needs a small home situated so she can walk to church and to the shops. Papa, I thought you might know of something available for rent."

Grandpa rubbed his chin for a few moments. "Don't know of anything right now. Heard the Bartletts want to sell. You might work out something with them."

He faced Petra. "Nice place and it's well-kept. They're leaving the furniture and going to live with their son in San Antonio."

Austin also faced Petra. "That is a sweet house. Would you like to talk to them?"

Interest softened her face. "Ja, and having furnishings would save money."

Gran smiled at Petra. "When you're moved in, perhaps you'd come for tea to meet some of the other women from town."

Petra's face shone with hope. "I would like that very much. You are gracious to suggest this when we have just met."

Gran nodded imperially. "We think a lot of Clara. I'm sure we'll become friends too."

Petra glanced at Clara with surprise. "She is a good niece—like a daughter."

When bid their goodbyes, Clara hung back a moment to hug Gran and give her cheek a kiss. "Thank you for telling my aunt you would invite her for tea. She has been very lonely."

Gran's face registered a gentle, surprised expression. "No trouble at all. I'll see she gets acquainted while you're helping Daniel."

She kissed Grandpa's cheek. "Thank you for your help."

Grandpa chuckled and touched the spot she had kissed. "Turned out to pay a dividend."

She joined the others in the buggy and they went to see the Bartlett home.

The house was one block off the main street. A frame home painted gray with white trim, the house had a wide porch which accommodated a bench and chair with plenty of room. The yard was fenced with wrought iron and had a concrete walk from the gate to the porch.

Petra gazed at the home. "This is very pretty. The large trees must help in the summer as well as look nice."

The Bartletts acted delighted to have prospects.

Petra examined each room thoroughly while Mr. Bartlett gave them a tour. After seeing the parlor, dining room, kitchen with mud room, two bedrooms, and a back yard where there was a garden and cellar, Petra smiled and sighed. "I like this house. Perhaps we can come to an agreement."

Later, on the way back to the ranch, Austin chuckled. "Petra, I've never seen better haggling. Guess I should take you next time I buy or sell cattle."

Petra shook her head. "Too bad they would not rent to me but he was stubborn. At least he came down on the price of the home. I like the furniture very much and there are no stairs to climb. This is good."

Rebecca asked, "What will you do if Clara goes away?"

"I will sell and follow her. This is why I hoped to rent." Petra shrugged. "Oh, well, the house and furnishings were ideal for me. I will enjoy this place and make it my home for as long as Clara is in McClintock Falls."

Clara hugged her aunt's shoulders. "I loved the house. The place should be cozy and give you pleasure."

Petra leaned forward to speak over Austin's shoulder. "I am from a very old city and was surprised your parents founded this one. When you were small, were there no buildings?"

"Oh, yes. Not many but we had a mercantile, saloon, livery, blacksmith, and feed store. I don't remember what else but there were several houses. Papa had divided the town into lots and streets. He didn't charge much for the lots. He gave some away if the person didn't have much money and was someone he thought would be a good citizen."

Her aunt nodded as if she approved. "Are you an only child?"

"Had a brother named Houston who died a little over fifteen years ago. His son Dallas was twelve and came to live with us and is like our son. I'm sure you'll soon meet the entire family."

"Oh, I would enjoy that."

Clara chuckled. "They took in their nephew Dallas as you and Uncle Hans did me. Theirs is a large extended family. Daniel wrote them down and how they're related. I'll show you the chart he drew when we are in my room."

***

Daniel massaged his temples, willing the headache to flee. What was taking Clara so long? Damn, he hated being stuck here. He loved his home, but not being able to leave made it his jail.

He hit the mattress with fisted hands. Of course he realized his vanity kept him here. With the Bath chair, he could be loaded into the buggy or wagon like so much freight and go places. Yeah, and have people gawk as if he were a carnival sideshow or pity him. Getting him in and out of the wagon would be a major production. No, thank you, he would walk or stay here.

Had his friends forgotten him? A few had come right after the accident but he had made it clear he didn't want to be seen in this condition. He'd rather be lonely than pitied.

When he heard Clara return, the morning's tension fled and he was almost giddy with relief. Stupid to be so attached to and dependent on one person but there was no denying her effect on him. Already he thought of her as his other half, his soul mate.

She breezed into the room with a smile. "You had a bit of a vacation this morning so we'll have to work harder this afternoon."

"You missed lunch. Before we work, sit down and tell me what happened on your trip."

She sat at the foot of his bed and spoke quietly. "Through Grandpa's suggestion, Aunt Petra bought the Bartlett home. She wanted to rent, but Mr. Bartlett was even more stubborn than my aunt—something I thought could not exist. She did talk him down on the price, though, and the house comes fully furnished. Plus, they served us dinner during negotiations."

"Nice little place as I remember." He looked toward the door then back at her. When is she moving?"

"They asked a week to get moved. They're going to live with their son." She scooted forward and lowered her voice even more, "Daniel, when I got to my room last night, my aunt was in tears. She had realized I did not want her here and talked about how no one likes her and she has no friends. I was so embarrassed I had been that obvious."

"Yeah, so what did you do?"

"I assured her my reaction was from surprise at her arrival and that we should be near one another because we were each other's only family. I have even come to think that's true."

He held her hand in his. "Are you sure after the way she treated you?"

"While she was eating, she mentioned that her parents treated her the way she treated me and she thought that is the way all parents acted toward children. Only Hans ever showed her love and I do not think he was demonstrative."

His lips in a fine line, he considered her revelation. "Doesn't explain wanting you to go to an orphanage."

She shook her head. "No, it does not. I'll ask her tonight. In the meantime, you must work your legs."

He grinned. "Hey, this is my naptime." He patted the bed beside him. "Come take a nap with me."

She pretended shock. "I think not. If you need sleep, Sir, I will leave you to do so."

"Just for an hour or so. Then I'll work hard." What a fool he was, exhausted from the mental anguish of not having her near.

She flashed her saucy grin. "Promise?"

"Promise." He'd do about anything for her, but how could he convince her she was The One for him?

Chapter Twelve

Clara found her aunt in the parlor with Kathryn and Rebecca.

Kathryn was sitting in the wingchair by the fireplace. "I remember the Bartlett home is lovely."

"Ja, and no stairs to climb each day. I will get my exercise walking around town and in the garden. Already vegetables grow there."

Rebecca asked, "Do you know how to drive a rig?"

Her aunt's brow furrowed. "I do not know what that is. If rig means a buggy, the answer is no. I have always walked or ridden with someone else driving."

Kathryn's lovely smile shone. "If you ever need to rent one, the man who brought you here, Fred Brewster, rents them. I can show you how to drive a buggy if you wish."

Petra's eyes overflowed with tears. She pulled a handkerchief from her pocket and dabbed at her eyes. "I am fortunate that your family is so kind. I understand why Clara is so happy here."

A knock at the door interrupted their conversation. Rebecca went to answer. She soon returned.

"Mama, Mrs. Zimmerman's in labor and she needs you."

Kathryn rose and patted Petra on the shoulder. "I know you'll excuse me. A patient needs my help."

Petra surprised Clara. "Ja, you will make her feel better when you smile."

Kathryn chuckled. "What a nice thing to say. Rebecca, you'd better come with me to keep those five other children out of the way and corralled."

The two women left, hurrying toward the carriage house.

Clara left her chair and joined her aunt on the couch. "How are you feeling?"

Petra's eyes widened. "I am well but tired from my journey, thank you for asking. Still am I a little sick from grief. Hans was a good husband and I thought we kept no secrets from one another. Learning we had money in savings was a shock and made me wonder why he has never told me this."

Clara squeezed her aunt's hand. "Probably he wanted to insure that you would be well-cared for after his death or that you would both have enough to remain comfortable after he retired."

"Perhaps." Petra frowned. "I do not think he could retire, do you? I cannot imagine him not going to his office at the university."

"But, he was not old enough yet. Who knows how he would have felt in twenty years?"

Her aunt jutted out her chin. "I do not think he would change much."

"I wanted to ask you something while we are alone. When my parents had died and you and Uncle Hans came to get me, I overheard you saying you did not want me to come live with you but thought I should go to an orphanage. Why did you say that?"

Her aunt's eyes widened and she laid a hand at her throat. "Ah, what you must have thought all these years. I am sorry you heard. I apologized to Hans many times for saying those words. Frankly, I did not think I would be a good mother. I thought that an orphanage's staff would know how to take care of you and give you what you needed."

Clara shook her head. "Most orphanages are notoriously bad and the children are neglected."

Petra raised a hand elbow high and shook it from side to side. "At the time, I did not know this. Once at a meeting of our church women, we had a program on local orphanages. I was shocked, appalled. As soon as I saw Hans I apologized. If I had known you heard us, I would have apologized to you."

Petra grasped both Clara's hands. "You must not think you were unwanted. I knew I was not very maternal. As it turned out, you were a blessing to us. Hans and I had wanted children at first but none came. We thought we would never have them and I grew to think this was God's will for me."

"Why did I have to sleep in that tiny room at the top of the house? There were guest rooms on the second floor."

Petra leaned back to peer at Clara. "Do you not remember that you chose the room? When we brought you home, you were so sad you hardly spoke. We showed you through the house and you wanted to be in the top. You called it your princess tower."

Clara struggled to control her tears. "I had forgotten but now I recall that memory. Oh, Aunt Petra, for years I thought you put me there because you did not think I was worthy of one of the better rooms."

Petra placed her arm around Clara's shoulders. "My poor Clara. Always Hans and I were glad you were with us."

Clara sniffed and brushed at her eyes with her fingers. "We must make up for many years of poor communication."

Petra dabbed her eyes. "But now we are together and able to talk to one another honestly."

Clara hugged her aunt. "I am glad you are here."

Petra sniffed and smiled. "Ja, me too."

***

The next day, the dressmakers returned.

"Aunt Petra Jaager, this is Madame Thibodaux and her assistant, Sylvie. I'm sorry I do not know your last name, Sylvie."

Sylvie sent a quick glance to her employer. "Wellburn."

Clara kept an arm around her aunt's shoulders. "I'm pleased my aunt is moving to McClintock Falls. I hope you won't mind if she watches the final fitting."

"As you wish." Madame clapped her hands. "Proceed to the proper room. We have much to do today."

Petra exchanged amused looks with Clara as they led the way to the bedroom.

Sylvie laid the creation on the bed and carefully removed the protective muslin.

When the garment was exposed, Petra gasped. "*Dit is ongelofelijk!*"

Clara stared in wonder. "I agree, Aunt Petra. It is incredible. I'm so grateful to Gran and to Madame and Sylvie."

Madame snapped, "Try it on. Though certainly my creation is worthy, we do not have all day for your admiration."

Clara removed her uniform and stepped into the dress. The fabric flowed over her like none she had ever experienced. "The fit is perfect."

Petra touched her fingers to the skirt. "Ja, this is the dress of a lifetime. You look like a princess." She smiled. "Without a tower."

Madame snapped, "Nonsense. I can create others as wonderful

anytime you wish."

Petra pressed her lips into a fine line for a few moments. "I want a dress, Madame. I am in mourning, but I do not want to look like a drab church mouse."

Madame's dark eyes lit as if she visualized gold coins. "Wonderful. Remove your clothes to your chemise and I will measure you. Sylvie, fetch my tape."

The helper scrambled through a large bag she carried and produced the tape measure, a notebook, and a pencil.

Petra nodded toward the door. "You must show the others while Madame works on me."

Clara debated, but opened the door and closed it behind her. She glided to Daniel's room.

He sat up and his mouth fell open. "Damn, you look like an angel. Clara, you're the most beautiful woman I've ever seen."

"You have not seen any lately except your beautiful mother and equally beautiful sister."

He shook his head, his eyes wide with what she thought was awe. "Wouldn't matter."

Clara pressed a hand on the bodice's vee at her waist. "I will see if Kathryn and Rebecca have returned."

The two women she sought came into the house as she entered the parlor. Both stopped and gazed at her.

Appearing exhausted, Kathryn set down her medical bag. "You are a welcome sight for tired eyes. You look absolutely gorgeous."

Rebecca started to touch the skirt then pulled back. "I wouldn't want to soil the fabric. We rode in the buggy and did some errands and my gloves might have gotten dusty. Clara, you look like a fairy princess from a storybook."

Emma came into the room. "Oh, my word. Isn't that the prettiest thing you've ever seen?"

Clara couldn't suppress her elation. "I never thought I'd have such a dress. Gran outdid anything I could ever imagine. Now my aunt has decided to hire Madame to create something nice for her even though she is in mourning."

Kathryn nodded. "Good for Petra. Every woman who sees you wearing that will want Madame to fashion something for her.

Fortunately, Madame never copies one of her originals."

"Now I'd better get changed and go back to the real world. I don't want Daniel to laze for too long." She walked slowly toward her room.

Madame and Sylvie were about to leave. "Since you are moving to town, Mrs. Jaager, I will see you there."

"You know where the Barlett home is?"

"I do. I'll send you a note to make sure the time is convenient." She nodded to Petra and to Clara. "I can show myself out."

Clara clasped her aunt's hands. "I am pleased you will have a new dress you did not have to sew."

Petra had dressed. "Turn and I will unfasten the buttons. I think she does not realize you do not have a lady's maid."

"Lucky I have you, isn't it?"

Petra's smile faded. "Please explain to me why this Gran person decided to give you the dress?"

Clara explained about the fireworks and her ruined dotted Swiss.

"This is kind of Gran. Always I liked that dress. Perhaps I can repair it while you work with your patient."

"That would be kind, Aunt Petra. I like the dress, too. Do you remember when we purchased the fabric and trims?"

Petra smiled. "Ja, with your first paycheck. Hans would not let you pay toward the food so you could not wait to have a new dress. We had a nice day, didn't we?

Clara met her aunt's gaze in the mirror. "We'll have many more happy days as well."

***

Two days later, Daniel leaned on the bars, experiencing a strange sensation. Could it be? He focused on moving his foot. Doing so required his complete concentration and effort.

Clara looked up at him. "Did you do that?"

He couldn't hold back a grin. "Do what? You mean this?" He moved the other leg.

She squealed, leaped up, and hugged him. He leaned down and captured her mouth. Their kiss heated his blood. Frustrated because he couldn't release the bars, he ended the kiss.

She kept her arms around him, her beautiful face glowing with delight.

Petra appeared at the door. "Is this the way you do therapy?"

Clara didn't look at all embarrassed, thank goodness. She glided to her aunt and hugged her. "Aunt Petra, the most wonderful thing happened. Daniel made two steps."

Petra rolled her eyes. "The way you were carrying on I thought he had learned to fly."

Clara laughed, apparently still bursting with glee. "Please, would you find Kathryn and ask her to come and see?"

She smiled, which softened her words. "So now I am an errand girl. Ja, I will go." She shook her finger. "No more kissing your patient."

Daniel waited until the woman was gone from the room. "Don't listen to her. Kiss away all you want."

Instead, she clasped her hands in front of her chest as she returned to the bars and stood in front of him. "I'm so excited. You are going to walk on your own soon." She motioned him toward her. "Keep walking toward me."

His mother hurried into the room followed by Rebecca and Emma.

Mama was out of breath. "Is it true, Daniel? Show me."

"A lot of fuss for my tiny steps." He focused and took two more steps then two more.

When he reached the end of the bars, he turned and let his weight sag on the harness. "Whew, that's as tiring as digging ditches."

Clara hurriedly brought the wheelchair to him. "You deserve a ride after that workout." When he was seated, she unfastened the harness.

Emma's eyes were moist. "Daniel, you come into the kitchen. Let's all have a treat to celebrate."

"Sounds good to me." What he really wanted was a rest, preferably with Clara at his side. Since that wasn't on the menu, he'd take whatever sweet treat Emma devised.

They were seated around the table, laughing and eating cake and drinking milk when Pa came in.

He looked around as if perplexed. "Did I miss supper?"

That set them laughing again.

Mama rose and hugged Pa. Tears streamed down her face.

"Daniel took steps today. He was holding on to those bars and they were tiny steps, but he walked. Austin, our boy actually walked."

Pa gave Mama a big kiss and twirled her in a circle. "Yee Haw!"

He plopped on a chair and pulled Mama onto his lap. "Best news I've had in two years."

Daniel enjoyed seeing the love his parents shared. That's what he wanted for himself with Clara.

Not realizing his thoughts, Clara smiled at him. "This is wonderful news indeed. But, he must continue working on the bars. Eventually, he will not need the harness or the bars."

He put on his innocent face. "You always want me to do the work, don't you?"

"Of course. And now, my work will be easier because you can move your own feet. No more duck-walking backwards for me."

He grinned at her. "So you get a vacation, huh?"

"Not to be. Putting all your weight on the bars as you walk without the harness will make your shoulders very sore and tight. I must give you longer massages."

Emma flexed her shoulders. "My, that sounds wonderful."

Clara scanned those at the table. "I can give a massage to you also or anyone who wishes. I would need to do this while Daniel is resting so I do not take time away from him."

Rebecca tilted her head. "Could you teach me to give a massage?"

Clara laughed. "I will be happy to and you can practice on me."

Mama said, "That's a good idea. I want to learn also. I used what I know of the subject on Daniel's legs. But, I have seen you, Clara, and your movements are more thorough and skillful."

***

That night as they prepared for bed, Petra turned to Clara. "Do you think this massage is something I should learn?" She examined her hands.

"I'm sure you could but why would you? First, you must get moved into your new home. Then, you must meet some of the women in town and make friends. If you wish to help people, there are many opportunities in any community. You can visit the sick, take food to the needy, and support the town's civic functions."

"Ja, perhaps you are right. I have much to do. I am excited to live in my new home. Keeping house will be easier and so will walking to shops. I will miss the sight of the water, but not the fear of a flood."

"When we are with others, we must take care not to say we think things in Amsterdam were better or that we think people here should do such and such like we did there. I miss the water sometimes but there are other compensations."

"Ja, Clara, I understand what you are saying. I will be…," she pretended to curtsy, "warm and delightful." She even giggled. "I see how this family acts. Can you imagine Hans kissing me and swinging me around in front of others?"

Clara shook her head. "Yet, I know he loved you very much. He just didn't show his feelings as the members of the McClintock family do. Perhaps he didn't know how."

"Only when we were alone did he let his love show. I am trying to learn how people here act. I noticed the grandparents are more formal."

"Not Grandpa, but certainly Gran is. She is also formidable and the queen of the town's society. Maybe not now, but I'll bet she still holds much sway."

"She was nice to me. I hope she will remember to invite me to tea."

"If she forgets, invite her to tea with you."

An incredulous expression appeared on Petra's face. "What a good idea. I will."

***

When Red returned from town with mail, the family was sitting at the supper table. Austin accepted the mail with his thanks to Red then sorted through the parcels and envelopes.

"Here's one for you, Clara. Looks official."

She accepted the missive with curiosity. "Since my aunt is here, I wonder who would write to me."

Daniel said, "Opening it would be a good way to find out."

"If no one objects my foregoing good manners, I will do so even though we are at the table."

Austin gestured. "Go ahead. You know we won't mind."

Rebecca giggled. "Especially if you tell us what the letter is about."

Clara turned the envelope over and slit the seal. When she extracted the letter, she saw it was from a hospital in St. Louis.

Dear Miss Van Hoosan,

You have been highly recommended by Dr. de Wees in agreement with your colleagues in Amsterdam. Our hospital is expanding and we are setting up a mechanotherapy section as part of our new orthopedic wing. We would like to talk with you about joining our hand-picked staff of professionals.
Please reply to this letter and let us know about your availability.

Yours sincerely,
Louis Arnoldson, M.D.
Head of Orthopedics

Rebecca stared at her. "Well, are you going to share the secret?"

Clara's head spun with possibilities and she had difficulty focusing to speak. "It's... It's from a doctor in St. Louis who got my name from Dr. de Wees in Amsterdam. This Dr. Arnoldson wants to talk to me about joining the staff of a new orthopedic wing's mechanotherapy unit."

She looked up from the letter. "That doesn't mean they would choose me, of course, just that I am being considered. I imagine it will come to nothing. Besides, I will be working with Daniel for quite some time."

Petra beamed at her. "This is an honor, Clara. Now you do not have to wonder about where you would go next if you decide to leave here."

"Having choices is always nice." She sensed Daniel's eyes on her but couldn't bring herself to meet his gaze. She folded the paper and slid it back inside the envelope.

But, the prospect did not bring her the happiness she would have expected. When she had arrived here, concern about what she would do and where she would go after this assignment weighed heavy on her mind. Silly woman, now she hated the thought of leaving Daniel and his family. What was she to do?

That evening in their room, Petra got ready for bed. "That is a good offer from this doctor, is it not?"

Clara hung up her uniform. "Yes, but I do not know what I will decide. Of course, I will write him right away and tell him of my obligations here. That will probably end the matter as I am sure he wants someone immediately."

Petra shook her dress and laid it on a chair, ready for the morning. "Tomorrow night we each will be alone. I look forward to moving into my nice little house but I will miss seeing you each day."

Clara was able to answer truthfully, "As I will miss you, but I will visit when I can. I am excited for you and all the possibilities opening for you."

"Ja, I am filled with… warm feelings." Petra grinned at her.

"I know you miss Uncle Hans, as I do, but you will be happy in town. I am sure of this. You have seen from Kathryn how to make friends and keep them. Soon, you will be the toast of this small town." She pulled her gown over her head and tied the ribbons.

"Clara, I have something to say to you before we part tomorrow. I-I hope you will not be offended."

"Whatever you are thinking, please tell me."

Petra laid her fingers on Clara's arm. "You must be more professional toward Daniel. When he looks at you his eyes betray his amorous thoughts toward you."

Clara patted her aunt's hand. "That's not uncommon for a patient in therapy. After they are healed, the attraction fades."

Petra went to her side of the bed and turned back the covers. "I see. And what of yours to him?"

Stunned, Clara had to wait a few seconds to answer. "D-Do I act as if I have amorous feelings for him?"

"Ja, but only to someone who has known you for twelve years. You must plan how to handle this, especially if you believe his attraction to you will fade when he is healed. Otherwise, you could be badly hurt or humiliated." Petra crawled between the sheets.

Clara placed a hand on her cheek and felt the heat of her blush. "Aunt Petra, I am embarrassed that you noticed what I have tried hard to hide. I have treated handsome men before but never have I been attracted to one of my patients. I assume this will also fade." She hoped so, but believed hers was a once-in-a-lifetime feeling.

"I will say no more about it now that you are warned. Time will tell. Do not allow sentiment to ruin an important opportunity and derail your career."

"I will not. This is something I must consider carefully."

What was she to do? If her aunt noticed, others might also.

Chapter Thirteen

Daniel wrestled with his improved function. As joyous as the ability to move his feet even for small steps was, exhaustion claimed him. Other things concerned him more right now.

Pa came in and sat at the foot of his bed. "Well, we got the aunt moved into her home. She's happy as if it were the grandest place in town."

"Her former home was three or four stories and always cold, according to Clara."

"She and Clara sure seem to be getting along well, considering how Clara was upset when her aunt showed up here unannounced."

"They talked out their differences and are close now. Too bad they had misunderstandings which made them both unhappy for years."

"Glad you're making progress, Son. I can't even imagine how hard this must be for you, but you'll get there. Anything I can do to help?"

Daniel glanced at the door to be certain they wouldn't be overheard. "Reckon you're the only one I can tell, Pa. Much as I hate to ask you to spend more on me, I sure would like one of those commode chairs. You know the kind I mean?"

"Like the one in your mother's and my room—looks like an oak armchair, but you can raise the seat and there's a hole to a chamber pot, right?"

"That's the kind. And a screen to give me some privacy would be appreciated. Guess I shouldn't complain, but using the bedpan is hard as hell since I can't lift my hips and have to rest on my fists. I tell you it's plumb embarrassing. I know Clara is professional and doesn't think twice about such things, but I do and feel mighty weird going in front of her. And, anyone could walk in."

Pa plowed his fingers through his hair. "Sorry we didn't think of something like that ourselves. Of course you're entitled to some privacy.

I'll see you have them tomorrow."

Pa paused then looked him straight in the eye. "Son, seems like you've become awful attracted to Clara."

Daniel's face heated and he hated that his tan had faded so much a blush would be obvious. He cleared his throat. "What if I have?"

Pa's hands came up palm forward. "No need to get riled. We've become real fond of her, too. But, remember she plans to move on after you're walking well."

"I know that's what she's said. But, I figure she could have a clinic in McClintock Falls as easy as anywhere. Hate to sound selfish but I'm sure upset that doctor in St. Louis had to stick in his nose with an offer at a fancy hospital."

Pa tsked. "Must be mighty tempting to her."

"With her aunt settled in town, I reckon that might help convince her to stay." The rosy picture Daniel had built disintegrated. "Hell, I'm dreaming. No reason she'd stay in a small town for a wreck of man like me."

"Hey, you're talking crazy. Don't talk down about yourself."

"She'd have to build a clinic here and get the word out. Would be lots of work when that doc offered a place already set up with the latest equipment."

"Doesn't hurt to plan as long as you realize she has worthwhile alternatives. After all you've been through, your mother and I sure don't want you hurt again." Pa patted his leg.

Daniel looked up and his face broke out in a smile. "Pa, I felt your hand when a week ago I wouldn't have. There's hope after all."

"If you could build a house with hope, we'd have us a fine palace. Nice to know our dreams are coming true. I'll see about the screen and chair. You keep working." He stood. "Whatever happens with Clara, remember your mother and I are on your side."

"I know you are and I can't tell you how grateful I am for all you and Mama have done. Josh and Dallas, too."

"That's what families do. See you later."

No sooner had Pa left than Clara came in. "Aunt Petra's completely moved in and incredibly pleased. The Bartletts left many of their things in addition to furniture."

"Guess their son won't have room for them otherwise."

Clara had a wistful expression. "Seems a shame to have to leave so much, and must be hard to bear. Aunt Petra had to do the same, though"

"Have you answered that St. Louis doctor's letter?"

She smiled and came closer. "Yes, and mailed it while I was in town. Why?"

He'd tried to think of a subtle way to find out, but he couldn't. "What did you tell him?"

She grinned and put her hands on her shapely hips. "Well, aren't you Mr. Nosey? And you think curiosity is a woman?"

"Aw, Clara, just tell me."

She sat on the foot of his bed. "If you must know, I told him I'm not available because I have a patient I can't dismiss for several weeks, possibly months."

He frowned at her. "You want to go live in St. Louis?"

"Daniel, I have to live somewhere."

"You could live here." Damn, he sounded like a kid. He hadn't intended to say it quite like that.

"I am trained to help people. Other than helping you, I cannot do that without a clinic or hospital and equipment."

"Tell me your dream situation—I mean if you could have anything you wanted."

She took a deep breath. "I have dreamed of having my own clinic like a sanitarium or small hospital and my own staff. I would have lovely rooms for the patients, with only one patient per room if possible. A gymnasium-like place for therapy would be next to a bathing pool with heated water. Park-like grounds around the clinic would allow the patients to enjoy fresh air in beauty."

"Hmm, sounds like you've given this a lot of thought."

She shrugged. "Ja, I am a good dreamer. Not so good at making dreams come true I guess."

"Did you dream of coming to America?"

Her expression brightened. "Ja, for several years that had been a dream."

"You made that one come true."

She waggled her forefinger at him. "No, your parents and Dr. Sullivan made it come true. I was lucky."

"I don't agree. If you hadn't worked hard and won the respect and admiration of your professors, you wouldn't have been recommended."

She tilted her pretty head. "Perhaps it was a combination. Whatever the reason, I am very glad to be here."

"And I'm especially grateful to have you here. Not only have you helped me, you've won the respect and admiration of my family and my love."

Her eyes widened. "Promise me you won't say that again, Daniel. We agreed you would wait until you were well and able to see other young women."

He chuckled as he shook his head. "Oh no, that was your suggestion. I never agreed."

She snapped, "Daniel McClintock, you are so stubborn."

Rebecca stood in the doorway. "I agree but what brought that on?"

He stared at his little sister, who was a pest right now. "Isn't anything private around here?"

"Not if you leave your door open and talk loudly. Mama wants you both to come for supper."

***

Clara helped Daniel from the harness. "Good job today. You are getting steadier each day."

"If your workouts don't kill me first, I'm going to walk on my own."

"Tomorrow, we will not use the harness. You did not need it today."

"Hey, I'll fall without support."

"You will not. Your arms and shoulders will get tired and sore—more than they are now. But, you will not fall."

"What if I want to fall?"

"Now you are being ridiculous. Instead of being silly, get ready for your massage."

"Sounds good to me. Your massages are the highlight of my day." He lay on his stomach.

"Rebecca is doing well at learning the technique. Having her practice on me is wonderful."

"I'll bet. Ah-h-h, that spot is especially sore. Did you know President George Washington spent two hundred dollars on ice cream the summer of 1790?"

She loved his odd items of history. "My goodness, he must have really loved ice cream."

"Imagine how much money that would be now almost a hundred years later. Probably it was the Treasury's money anyway and not his own."

Clara tried to remember something to surprise him. "Did you know the stage before frostbite is called frostnip?"

"Had no idea. Did you know that the equal sign was invented in 1557 by Welsh mathematician Robert Recorde who was tired of having to write 'is equal to' over and over?"

"I suppose you know that because you keep the ranch's books and the fact is related."

"Nope, simply read it somewhere and though it interesting."

"I am glad you read. Reading improves the mind, but not if you only learn items that are not helpful."

"Nothing learned is ever wasted. For instance, when I learned that I saved it for such an occasion as this."

"Sometimes I think you are a bit crazy."

He raised his head to look at her. "But adorable, right?"

"Baby Austin is adorable. You are incorrigible."

"Ha, I'll bet you learned that word in English class and have been biding your time and wanting to use that word."

"What word? Baby Austin?"

"That's two words. You know I meant incorrigible. That must be hard for someone new to English."

"Hard words are those that begin with TH or W. You must roll onto your back now." She helped him turn.

"Your English has improved since you've lived here."

"Speaking every day with you and your family has helped me. I am not learning Spanish as quickly."

"You're right, we don't spend enough time practicing. I think we should have a specific time to devote to our language lessons."

"Teaching me Spanish is a much better use of your time than thinking of things like George Washington's ice cream."

***

Clara found Kathryn in her herbal studio while Daniel napped. "He can walk, but he won't let go of the bars. He's afraid he'll fall. I don't know if he's afraid he will hurt himself or embarrass himself."

Kathryn grimaced and continued to crush herbs with a mortar and pestle. "Knowing my son, probably both."

"Having him refuse to walk even a few steps on his own is frustrating. The truth is he won't walk as well as before the accident, but he will walk."

Kathryn looked up from her labors. "You mean he'll be shaky and his movements slow?"

"Not exactly. His gait will have changed. Have you seen a music box with a moving figure?"

"Rebecca has a music box like that which the boys got her for her thirteenth birthday." Kathryn raised her hand in the air. "When the lid opens, a beautifully dressed woman walks around with a bird perched on her hand. They ordered the gift from New York, but the label says France. I'm sure it was expensive but it's lovely."

"Then you understand. Instead of a smooth gate, his is more like an automaton. He hates that he cannot move smoothly and rapidly. Of course, he will continue to improve for many months before his walk becomes static."

Kathryn poured the herbs she had just ground into a pottery jar. "He has always held himself to the highest standards of performance. From the time he was small, he wanted to do everything as well as Josh. The difference between them is that Daniel was shy and read a lot."

Clara grinned at the other woman. "He still reads a lot." More seriously, she added, "He insists he cannot walk without support. I will continue trying to convince him he can walk on his own."

Kathryn set down the jar and hugged Clara. "Thank you, Clara, for all you've done. You've been such a blessing as well as a good friend."

"What a kind thing to say. Thank you."

***

Daniel frowned and looked at Clara. "What's that noise? What's going on out there?"

"Nothing to concern you right now. Keep walking toward me."

He bent sideways over the bar to look out the window. "What are Red and Lucky building?"

"Something I asked for. You can see when they have completed the project."

"Clara, explain."

"I cannot for it is something you must see. I do not know the English words for their construction."

"But you know words like construction and incorrigible. I think you're hiding something. You promised you would always tell the truth."

"All right. I dawdled... is that a word for prevaricated?"

"No, but so you lied. About what?"

Red knocked on the window. "All finished, Miss Van Hoosan."

"Thank you very much, Mr. Nunn and Mr. Dixon."

"Now will you tell me?"

She positioned his chair so he could sit down. "Better than that, I will show you."

He maneuvered into the Bath wheelchair. "This had better be good."

"I believe it is wonderful. You will see, ja?" She pushed the chair through the hall, parlor, and foyer.

When she reached around him to open the front door, he grabbed the wheel rims and tried to stop her from shoving him outside. From this angle, she was stronger and prevailed. The chair bumped over the threshold and he was on the front porch.

Then, he saw what the noise had been. A gently sloping ramp had been built from the porch to the ground. What the hell was she thinking?

"You know I don't want to be in this chair where anyone but family can see me. Why would you do this me?"

"Do you think the men who work here are unaware of you? Don't you think they care what happens? Let me assure you they know your progress and are eager to help."

The knowledge the ranch hands knew what he'd been doing and how well heightened his frustration. "So what? You let me turn this around and go back inside."

Clara proceeded as if she were oblivious to his complaints. "You cheat them by shutting them out. You have also cheated yourself of time out of doors. We are going for a short walk then I will take you inside."

His body tensed until his muscles quivered. "Clara, you have no right to do this."

"This is part of your treatment. Do you remember when I told you about my dream clinic and said a pretty garden for fresh air and sunshine?"

"That was a fantasy. This is real. You shouldn't do this to me."

"Ja, I am the therapist and this will help you. You must trust me."

"I did trust you. Now I'm not so sure."

"Do not lie to me, Daniel. Does it not feel good to be outside again? Have you not missed being able to leave the house?"

He hated being trapped inside, but he'd come to think of his room as his world. "That's not the point. You are forcing me to do something I specifically told you I didn't want to do."

"Ja, but you did not want to try the parallel bars either. Look how that turned out. Now you can walk."

The fact she had a point failed to decrease his ire. "Where the hell are we going?"

"Up to the main road and then back. I think that will be a good start for you. Tomorrow we can go further if you wish."

"I won't wish. You won't be able to trick me out here tomorrow." He'd show her how uncooperative he could be.

"Daniel, stop fussing and look around you. The sky is bright blue, there is a gentle breeze to cool us, and the sun is shining. Listen to the birds serenading us, rejoice in being alive on such a fine day."

"You're a bully, Clara Roos Van Hoosan."

She leaned near his ear. "If you don't like where I am pushing the chair then get out and walk."

"That's not funny. Walking is hard enough with the bars to support me. I can't walk without that prop."

He peered ahead. "Looks like Roy Evans is taking horses for Dallas and Finn to train. He ought to have them on a string. Looks like they're free."

Something on the road must have frightened the horses. The bay in back whinnied and darted forward. As he passed the other two, they joined in the run. Roy and his son Harley tried to cut off the horses without success.

"Clara, we need to get behind a tree. Those horses are headed this way."

She didn't move. When he turned to look at her, her face was a mask of terror. If they didn't move now, they'd be trampled.

He stood and stepped in front of her, waving his arms and yelling, "Heeyaw, heeyaw!"

The horses turned and ran toward the barn. Harley and Roy had lassos ready but couldn't get in a position to throw the ropes. Near the barn, Lucky opened the corral gate and the horses galloped into the corral.

Daniel grabbed Clara's shoulders. "You're all right. The horses are penned."

She blinked and grabbed his arms. "Daniel, you are walking. You walked to save us—to save me. I thought I was going to die like my parents. I was so frightened I could not move."

The realization slammed into him. He'd only made a few steps, but he'd risen from the wheelchair and stepped in front of Clara. She'd insisted for three days that he could walk without support if he tried.

He embraced her. "Looks like you were right. I can walk at least a few steps without the bars. Are you okay?"

She rested her head against him. "My chest does not want me to breathe and my heart is racing faster than those horses ran. Thank you for saving me."

"My legs want me to sit down. I can wheel myself and you walk beside me. You need to get something from Mama for shock."

"Ja, we will go back to the house now. I did not mean to come this far but you were arguing with me and I kept walking."

Harley rode up, reining in about ten feet away. "Daniel, Paw and me are sure sorry we scared you folks. Damn…begging your pardon, Ma'am, one of those darn horses went crazy when a rabbit jumped onto the road. That's why we want Dallas to train them."

Daniel sat back in the wheelchair. "He can get them to do what he wants. He talks to them like they were people and they seem to understand. You'll be pleased with the results."

"Well, I'd better get back and help Paw. Nice to see you again, Daniel." He touched two fingers to his hat brim. "Ma'am." He turned and sent his horse and galloping toward the corral.

Clara still pushed him even though he could have managed on his own. He didn't argue because he figured she'd had enough to contend with for one day.

She walked slowly. "I was so frightened I couldn't move or speak. My legs went weak and I was dizzy. I thought I would fall and be trampled."

"The event is over so try to put it your of your mind."

"Daniel, if I live to be a hundred, I will never forget that experience. I am sure I will have nightmares tonight. Worse, you could have been trampled. After all your hard work, you could have been even worse."

"Think of something else."

He searched his memory for something to distract her. "Did you know that some people used to believe tomatoes were poisonous? In 1820 this man named Robert Johnson in Salem, New Jersey brought a bunch of them in front of the courthouse and ate tomatoes in front of a crowd. The people in the crowd waited for him to die, but he didn't."

"I imagine they were surprised. Do you not believe that is kind of ghoulish of the crowd?"

"Now that you mention it, I do. Did you know that in Japan it's considered good manners to slurp and burp while eating?"

"Are you sure that is correct?"

"Yes, Ma'am."

"Then you would do well in Japan."

"Hey, there's nothing wrong with my table manners. Even though we usually eat in the kitchen, Mama insists each of us learn the niceties."

"I apologize because you are correct. Kathryn must have a secret way to convince you to follow her rules."

"Yep. Growing up if we didn't act properly, we had to leave the table. A couple of times missing a meal was a good lesson. Not that we missed many, you understand. Mama made sure we ate well."

Once inside the house, they returned to his room. "That bed has never looked more welcoming."

Clara waited until he was in bed. "While you are resting, think how you want to let your family know you have walked. This will be a wonderful surprise."

"Okay. You need to rest too."

"Ja, I have barely enough energy to get to my bed and lie down. I will check on you in an hour or so."

Chapter Fourteen

Clara had never been so weak. Her legs threatened to become rubber and did not want to follow her commands. She managed to remove her shoes then she laid on the bed to rest. Perhaps she could sleep for an hour.

She awoke from a nightmare to the chatter of voices coming from the parlor. When she checked her lapel watch for the time, she was appalled. She had slept for three hours. What must the McClintocks think?

She rose and washed her face and hands. After smoothing her hair, she put on her shoes. Now she had to face the family. She hoped they were not angry with her for neglecting her duty.

When she reached the parlor, she was ready to explain her carelessness with Daniel's life. Instead of censure, the family members swarmed around her.

Kathryn had been crying. "You did it, Clara. Daniel walked and it's thanks to you. I know he needs more therapy, but he got up from his wheelchair and walked to me." Tears pooled in her eyes.

Austin hugged her. "Young lady, you are worth your weight in gold."

Emma dabbed at her eyes. "I knew he would walk. I'm so happy our boy is healed."

The love and kindness shown in this room amazed Clara. This must be the nicest family in the world. She savored their praise even though she was simply doing her job—the one this family paid her to do.

"I thought you would be angry that I took such a long nap and neglected my duties with Daniel. That you are not upset is such a relief to me."

Austin shook his head. "Daniel explained what happened. With your family background, you must have been terrified."

Kathryn took her hand. "We waited supper for you. Let's go into the kitchen now and eat."

Daniel was back in his wheelchair. "I'm starving. Clara makes me work so hard I need lots of food."

In the kitchen, Clara sank onto the chair she had come to think of as hers. "You must not complain. Working hard is why you can walk. We will continue working until you no longer need the wheelchair. If you wish, you may use a cane."

Daniel's raised his eyebrows. "I don't intend to use a cane."

Rebecca spread her napkin across her lap. "I think a cane makes a man look sophisticated, debonair."

Daniel looked at his sister. "That's because in those romance novels you read the hero often carries a cane."

"How do you know? You can't have gone up to my room to steal mine."

"I heard you and your friend Maddie talking about them."

Her eyes were round as saucers and she looked aghast. "You eavesdropped?"

"I didn't move. If you giggly girls talk loud enough that I can hear you in my room, you can't accuse me of intentionally listening."

"You could have warned us."

Kathryn clapped her hands. "Silence both of you. We will have a big celebration next Friday night and Josh and Dallas and their families will be here. Of course I'll invite Petra and Gran and Grandpa, too. Maybe we'll invite the O'Neill, McDonald, and Clayton families and have a cèilidh."

Clara clasped her hands at her waist. "When I was a little girl, my parents and I sometimes went to our Scottish neighbor's for a cèilidh. They were such fun."

Daniel wriggled on his chair. "Mama, don't you think you should wait to celebrate until I can walk across the room at least? I don't think wobbling a few steps qualifies."

Kathryn jutted out her jaw. "It does to us."

***

As soon as they had finished breakfast the next morning, Clara pushed him to his room. "We had better get very busy. You must walk as well as possible for your party. More, you must do this for yourself."

"Did I tell you that you look your usual beautiful self this morning?"

"A woman can never hear that too often." She removed the harness apparatus and laid it aside. "I will put this in one of my trunks."

"Don't leave me."

She met his gaze. She knew what he meant but pretended otherwise. He should be ecstatic at his improvement and not thinking of her.

"I will be right here, Daniel. The loop goes around your waist as usual. If you start to fall I will catch you. But, if you know you are falling, grab the bars."

He loosely held her wrist. "I mean don't leave me now that I can walk."

"You are not completely rehabilitated yet. I am still your therapist. Now that you can walk, there are additional exercises you must learn. Do not think of anything but walking, especially until your party. Go and walk between the parallel bars without touching them."

"Yes, Master." He needed no assistance to reach the bars.

Clara was elated to realize Daniel no longer had to focus so diligently to walk. In another way, his progress made her sad. She loved being here and loved him. Soon he would not need her and there would be no reason for her to stay. She could live with Aunt Petra, but that was not a satisfactory solution.

Just when she had decided he no longer needed the bars, his legs folded. He pulled her down with him. She held the loop but he was dead weight.

She rose and flexed her shoulders and back. "Grab the bars and pull yourself up."

He remained in a crumpled heap. "I'd love to do the baboon thing, but I can't. My muscles froze and I'm helpless as a newborn baby. Give me a minute or two and hope I recover."

"Has this ever happened to you before now?"

"Jumping out of the wheelchair yesterday might have been too much for me even though it was necessary. I'm fine, though. The feeling is coming back."

The idea of him having another of these attacks terrified Clara. How could she prepare him for something she didn't understand? They needed to tell Dr. Sullivan about this episode.

Rebecca came in. "What's wrong? Daniel, are you hurt?"

"I'm fine. Had a little setback. Give Clara a hand to help me up, will you?"

With Rebecca's help, Clara got Daniel on his feet. He stood between the parallel bars and slowly walked toward the end. She held the belt firmly. Instead of turning to go the other direction, he walked to the bed, laid down, and exhaled deeply.

Clara knew something must be hurting in spite of him saying he was fine. She stood beside his bed and used her most professional tone, "Daniel, are you injured?"

He gave her a sheepish look. "Maybe a little. If you're not hurt, reckon I could have my massage of these crazy muscles now?"

That confirmed to Clara that he had been injured. "Of course."

Rebecca followed her. "You're limping, Clara."

Clara smiled at the girl. "I am fine, just a little bump." Actually, her left side hurt—ankle, knee, and hip.

Rebecca narrowed her eyes. "I know I'm not as good as you are. Just the same, when you've finished my brother's massage, I'm giving you one."

Clara sighed. "I will not turn you down."

***

The next day when Red brought the mail, she had another letter from Dr. Aronson. She opened it with trembling fingers.

Dear Miss Van Hoosan,
Because of a medical conference, I will be in your area on the tenth. I hope I may call on you at the McClintock Ranch. I look forward to meeting you in person.
Sincerely yours,
Louis Arnoldson, M.D.

Daniel glared at her. "What does he say?"

She looked at Kathryn. "Dr. Arnoldson is going to be here on the tenth and would like to call on me here. I do not have time to respond by mail and I cannot send him a wire because he did not say where his conference will be held. I apologize if you do not want him to call here."

Kathryn glanced at Daniel then her. "Of course you may have him visit here. I'm sure he wants to talk you into leaving rural life for the big city."

"I have not decided what I will do when Daniel no longer needs therapy. He is doing well and I am very happy for him."

"I'm in the room, Clara. You don't have to speak about me as if I were somewhere else or too dumb to understand what you're saying."

Clara whirled. "You are not dumb but you are the most obstinate person I have ever met. Instead of rejoicing because you can walk, you are complaining."

"I'm happy I can walk. But, I think you should stay in McClintock Falls instead of racing off to St. Louis."

"Did you not hear me say I have not decided? There are many things to consider."

Kathryn came to stand beside Clara. "In a few minutes I'm going to town. Why don't you come with me and visit your aunt and shop?"

"I would love to." Her burst of excitement evaporated. "Oh, no, thank you. This is the time for Daniel's therapy."

Kathryn chuckled. "I hardly think one afternoon will halt his recovery."

"If you are sure, please let me change clothes quickly." Clara hurried to her room.

She had a dress ready for just such an opportunity. The dress was one she copied from the trousseau of Princess Beatrice three years ago. Dark red habit cloth with ottoman silk of the same shade formed the vest. The garment was simple and tasteful in design and she felt like a princess when she wore it.

When she emerged from her room, Daniel waited in the parlor.

"You're beautiful." His eyes conveyed his admiration.

"Thank you. Shall I bring you something from town?"

He mulled over the question. "I sure would like some horehound candy. And see if they've had a new shipment of books. I've about memorized the ones we have."

"I certainly will."

Kathryn anchored her hat with another hatpin. "Shall we go?"

They reached town quickly. Kathryn left the buggy at the livery stable.

She linked her arm with Clara's. "Why don't we go to your aunt's house first? Then, if she has something planned for today, we'll have time to arrange a later visit."

"That sounds logical. I am eager to learn how she is getting on in her new home."

When they arrived at Petra's house, she was pulling weeds from the front flower beds.

As they reached the gate, Clara called, "Aunt Petra, you have visitors."

When Petra looked up, a huge smile appeared on her face. "I must be magic because I was just thinking about you. Come in and we will have tea."

When they were inside the kitchen, Clara hugged her aunt before taking a seat at the table. "How have you been?"

Petra was more animated than Clara had ever seen her. Her aunt took a tea kettle and filled it with water before setting on the range. "Many things have happened. Zarelda invited me for tea. Because of her generosity, others also have invited me."

"You didn't have to ask her first then. That's good news."

Petra measured tea into the teapot. "I have been to church and attended a meeting of the women."

Kathryn nodded. "What did you think of them?"

"I liked them. They do not just gossip. They make quilts for the needy and also take food to the sick. You know I enjoy sewing and I said I would help with quilts. The quilt group will come here on Tuesday so I want everything to look perfect."

Petra grabbed Kathryn's hand in both of hers. "I am a success because I have pretended I was you each time I meet people. Because of you, I know how to act warm and friendly."

Kathryn's smile lit her face. "Petra, what a nice thing to say. I'm pleased you're making friends."

Petra poured steaming water into the teapot to steep. She set out the dishes and utensils they would need.

"Aunt Petra, that's wonderful news. What can I do to help?"

"Not a thing." She paused in pouring tea. "On second thought, perhaps you can walk through the house and see if there is anything out of place or that I haven't cleaned."

"I will be happy to. After tea, I will help you pull weeds."

Her aunt's eyes widened. "In that dress, you will not. I have several days to prepare and there is not that much left to do. On Monday, I will bake."

She jumped up. "I forgot to serve you pound cake."

They chatted for half an hour.

Kathryn set her empty tea cup on its saucer. "I'm enjoying this, but I have errands at Roan's Mercantile. You ladies are invited to join me if you care to." She rose. "Petra, thank you for a lovely time. Next time I will bring the cake."

Petra looked at Clara. "What do you prefer?"

Clara shrugged. "I came to visit with you so we will do what you wish, but I did promise Daniel I would look for a new book… and some candy." She grinned at Kathryn.

Petra stood. "Let us shop and we can visit on the way. You look too nice to hide inside. Kathryn, do you mind waiting while I get my purse and tidy my hair?"

Clara basked in the company of her two favorite women. How sad to think she and Petra could have shared joy-filled times these past twelve years if they had understood one another. Thank goodness, Kathryn and Rebecca were close

When Petra rejoined them, she had changed dresses and wore a hat.

Kathryn's eyes conveyed excitement. "Daniel has taken steps unaided. Of course, he still needs a lot of help from Clara. We're having a big party Friday and we hope you'll come. You will need a ride. I'm sure you can come with Gran and Grandpa."

Petra's brown eyes lit with delight. "I would like this very much. I am glad your Daniel is improving. You must be very pleased."

Kathryn practically danced when she walked out of Petra's home. "Austin and I are over the moon happy. Plus, for the first time in two years, Daniel has regained his hope."

Clara took her aunt's hand. "Did you bring your wooden clogs?"

"Ja, even though I could not imagine I would wear them here, I hated to leave them behind."

"Bring them to the party. It is to be a cèilidh with music and dancing. We will show the Irish dancers how the Dutch dance."

"I will also bring my cap." Her aunt pondered a few moments. "I have not danced in many years. I may not remember how."

"You will. Only a little bit, we don't have to put on an entire show. I would like for others to see something of Amsterdam and The Netherlands."

"Ja, this will be fun."

Kathryn waved at the doctor. "John, wait a moment." They crossed the street, which was unpaved.

Dr. Sullivan's smile welcomed them. "What are you three lovely ladies up to today?"

Kathryn took his arm and they walked together while Clara and her aunt followed.

"John, we're having a party Friday to celebrate Daniel taking steps unaided by the bars. You were instrumental in his progress by finding Clara. Please say you'll come."

"He's taking steps now? I wouldn't miss the chance to celebrate that for the world. I can't tell you how happy hearing this news makes me."

"We're having a large group and probably a cèilidh."

John stopped and turned to Petra. "Mrs. Jaager, perhaps you'd care to ride there with me and spare my going alone."

Petra's mouth moved but no words came out for a minute. "Ja, Doctor, I would enjoy that."

"Please, call me John. We're not formal here."

Petra blushed like a schoolgirl. "You must call me Petra."

He tipped his hat. "Good, Petra, I'll come by for you about six on Friday. Nice to have seen you ladies but I have patients to see." He went into his office.

Clara squeezed her aunt's hand. "That's wonderful. He will be interesting to talk to on the drive. Not that Gran and Grandpa wouldn't you understand, but you will enjoy knowing this kind man."

Kathryn's excitement kept her moving rapidly as they approached Roan's Mercantile. "Red does well with my list, but I have a few items I wanted to choose myself."

Clara peered around the store. "Go ahead. I also have things to find."

Petra wandered away so Clara headed for the books. She had perused the book titles in Daniel's room but hadn't studied those in the other parts of the house. She'd make choices and, if necessary, depend on Kathryn to help avoid duplication.

The store's book selection was small, but included some recently published novels. Clara had selected a couple when Mrs. Roan approached.

"May I help you, Miss Van Hoosan?"

Clara faced the storeowner. "You know who I am. Ah, there are not many tall Dutch newcomers, are there?"

Mrs. Roan smiled. "I saw you come in with Kathryn McClintock. Everyone has heard you've come to help Daniel and we're all so hopeful. Are those books for you or for him?"

"*Ramona* is for me. Do you know what he doesn't have yet?"

"He's quite the reader, but we have new arrivals since his family last purchased for him. He's read *Tom Sawyer*, but not *Huckleberry Finn* and they really are a pair that should both be read. *Study in Scarlett* is an exciting mystery by an author new to me, Arthur Conan Doyle. *The Canterville Ghost* is good—I have a copy."

Clara suppressed a giggle at the mention of *Tom Sawyer*, the book Daniel had thrown at her the first day. "I will take those. Are there others?"

"These by Robert Louis Stevenson, Jules Verne, and Thomas Hardy are books he'd enjoy, as would you. I think Daniel has *Mayor of Casterbridge* but not *The Woodlanders*. *Kidnapped* is supposedly a young person's story, but my husband and I enjoyed it."

"Then, I will take those also. He loves to read and so do Rebecca and I. In fact, these will bring enjoyment to all in the household. Daniel gets bored. Now that he is walking a bit, perhaps he will not be inactive."

Mrs. Roan's eyes lit and she clasped her hands to her chest. "I had not heard he's walking. Praise God! Oh, and you are also to receive some credit."

"The credit goes to God and Daniel. He takes only a few steps now, but I believe he will continue to improve."

"That's wonderful news. Is there anything else for you?"

Clara juggled the stack of books. "This is all I can carry but I also want a dime's worth of horehound candy and a nickel's worth of peppermints."

They walked to the store's counter where Kathryn and Petra waited with their packages.

Kathryn stared at Clara's load. "My goodness, did you buy all of the books? Be sure and put them on our account."

"Mrs. Roan helped me select several that Daniel has not yet read. A couple of books are for me, but others in the family might enjoy them too. I wish to pay for them myself from the generous salary you give me."

Petra sent Clara a knowing look. She stepped closer and whispered, "This is the way you act professional with your patients?"

Clara disregarded her aunt and paid for the candy and books. "Do you have other errands, Kathryn?"

Kathryn took one of the book packages. "Let me treat us to lemonade at the diner before we go home."

While they waited for their drink, Clara asked her aunt, "Have you found the solicitor's letter yet?"

Her aunt's shoulders dropped. "I am embarrassed. The van der Mere's were already cutting a hole in the wall when I was packing. I dumped all the papers I thought I would need plus photographs and small paintings into the bottom of my largest trunk. Such a mess I have but I will get them sorted eventually

Clara wanted to speak sharply so she held her tongue. One day, perhaps she could go to her aunt's and help sort through the papers.

Later, on the way to the ranch, Kathryn glanced at Clara. "You were generous to pay for those books yourself. You should have put them on our family's account."

"I wanted them to be from me. Daniel has been working very hard and doing all I have asked. Sometimes he pretends to grumble, but actually he is trying as hard as possible to regain use of his legs. The rest of your family might enjoy the books as well."

Kathryn sent her one of her sweet smiles. "That's kind of you. No wonder we think of you as one of the family."

Her remark warmed Clara. She would love to be a member of this wonderful family. Daniel's ardor was certain to cool once he was walking and exposed to women not in his family. She must guard her heart—but she feared she was too late.

Chapter Fifteen

Daniel was astonished by all the books. "I hoped for one. This is unbelievable." He munched a piece of candy from the bag.

Rebecca hurried in to pounce on the selection spread out on Daniel's bed. "Mama said you have books."

Clara gave her the bag of peppermints. "I did not forget you."

The girl hugged Clara. "Thank you. Which book should I read first?"

Clara handed her *Ramona*. "I really got this one for myself, but you read fast so I will wait until you are finished. Or, you might like to start with *Study In Scarlett*, which is a mystery."

Rebecca chose *Ramona*. "Bye, I'll see you when I've finished this and the peppermints."

She examined the remaining books. "I might have been carried away. I love to read and I know you do also. I couldn't resist. Too bad your town does not have a library."

"There's been talk of building one." He picked up *Huckleberry Finn*. "By Mark Twain, the same author as the one you stole."

She pretended to be insulted. "I did not steal *Tom Sawyer*, you gave it to me and I returned it as soon as I had read it."

"You live in a dream world, Clara Roos Van Hoosan, if you believe that. I won't argue, though, since you brought all of these."

"First, you must do exercises."

"Here's a surprise for you, Miss Van Hoosan. Rebecca watched me so I could practice walking between the bars. I exercised a long time then took a nap." He sent her a mischievous grin. "Did you know some snails have 1400 teeth and some can even kill you?"

She put her hands on her hips. "Who counted the teeth?"

He burst out laughing. "I wondered that myself."

Clara searched her memory to recall some odd fact to surprise him. "Did you know that Romans used to brush their teeth with urine?"

He pretended to gag. "I thought my tooth powder tasted bad. I won't complain about it again."

She gathered all but one book and stacked them on the chest of drawers across the room. "I doubt that. I believe you enjoy complaining."

He laid his hand over his heart. "How can you say that? I am the picture of reason and amiability." He smiled as if pleased with himself.

She set the book he had kept to read on the bedside table. "You have rested long enough. Get ready for your massage."

He stripped off his nightshirt. "Ah, your hands rubbing my skin, skimming over sensitive areas—I'm always ready for that, pretty lady."

She wanted to pinch him but resisted. "Do not pretend this has anything to do with male/female relations. This is strictly part of your treatment toward healing. Keep your mind centered on walking better."

He stretched out on his bed. "I do but there's no reason I can't enjoy the benefits of your massage, is there?"

Clara helped him turn over on his stomach. "I will work first on your back so I do not have to see your smirk."

"Do you have trouble reading books in English?"

She worked on his shoulders, which were knotted from work on the bars. "I read much slower than you. I have trouble with some words. Still, I enjoy reading in English more than German or French."

"There you go showing me up again. Soon you'll be reading in Spanish as well. Here I am stuck with only English."

She laughed at him pretending to feel outdone. "You have no need to read in languages other than English. I had to learn at school. If I had stayed in Amsterdam, that would have been useful. Here, I do not need that skill."

"I don't know, may come in handy sometime. We have a lot of nationalities here. There're a lot of German's in Texas and one or two German couples in town. Probably French around, too. A lot of people in Louisiana speak French as well as English."

She had not heard about the French. "I did not know this. How far is this Louisiana?"

"From here, I guess about five hundred miles."

She helped him turn over onto his back. "I have trouble conceiving the enormity of this country. I loved looking out the window of the train, at least until we were near here and I was too eager to arrive. Even then, I could not imagine that all I saw was one country. I do not know all the states' sizes."

"You'll learn." He met her gaze, his eyes dancing with mischief. "Did you know that medieval English longbows could fire an arrow further than three hundred yards?"

She shook her head. "Where do you get these odd facts? Hmm, let me see if I can remember one. Do you know that dolphins sometimes rescue stranded swimmers?"

"No, but then I've never seen a dolphin or the ocean."

That surprised her when she had grown up taking the sea for granted. "Is the sea far from here?"

"Gulf of Mexico is over two hundred seventy-five miles. I've had no reason to go there."

"That is far but at least there is a nice river near town."

"The Medina River, and it also runs through the ranch. I've seen that."

She laughed. "Of course you have."

"I've ridden across it and even gone swimming in the river. There's a good swimming hole on the ranch."

"Swimming hole?"

"Where the river forms a sheltered pool. Nice sloping beach on one side but the other side is hard to climb."

"When—if—I build my clinic, I will include an indoor pool with warm water for patients' exercises."

"Does Dr. What's-his-name's place have one?"

She ignored the snide part of his remark. "I do not know but I imagine so. You can ask Dr. Arnoldson when he comes."

He shook his head. "Oh no, not me. I won't speak to him. He's all yours."

"How nice of you to give this man to me. Do you not think he will have something to say about that?"

"Don't care what he thinks. He has his nerve coming here to try and steal you from us."

She changed her massage to his left leg. "Daniel, he is not stealing me from anything. Soon you will not need me to help you walk. You are doing very well and I am proud of you."

"Then stay here. You have a room and your aunt is here."

"Please be reasonable. I can't live in the room next door to yours forever. I can't live with my aunt forever either."

"I told you Pa will give you forty acres of the ranch down by the river. That's a real pretty sight. Peaceful, too."

She switched to his right leg. "And would I have my clinic in a tent?"

"Think about it, will you?"

"Your father is generous to offer the land. I will think about this place. Think is all I can do, though."

"Did you find out about your inheritance from your aunt? Maybe there's enough to build your clinic."

"I cannot imagine there is. My aunt is having trouble finding the papers. She is not used to conducting business and is unorganized. This is a surprise because always she kept her home immaculate and well managed."

"You should help her look."

"I will offer to do so but she is not likely to welcome interference."

"Damn, Clara, it's not meddling. The money is yours and you deserve to know how much there is."

She finished and moved to stand near him. "I will try, Daniel. Do not get upset with me."

He took her hand and guided her to sit on his bed beside him. "I'm not angry with you. I don't want you to leave me. I have money in savings from my share of the ranch profits and I can add that to whatever you have coming. We could be partners in the clinic and in life."

She framed his face with her hands. "You are a wonderful man, Daniel. When you are well and have been surrounded by other women, you will see that you no longer care for me as other than a friend. I cannot be locked into a partnership with a man who no longer cares for me."

He gripped her shoulders. "Listen to me. I will never stop loving you. You are the only woman I want or need by my side for the rest of my life."

Tears overflowed from her eyes. She laid her head on his chest.

"I want that to be true but I'm afraid. Patients have had crushes on me before until after they leave the clinic. Then their ardor fades quickly."

He cradled her, caressing her back. "Aw, sweetheart, don't cry. Please believe my love is genuine and won't lessen over time. Give me a chance."

She raised her head and pulled out her handkerchief and dried her tears and blew her nose. "It is time for your rest. Then we will get busy with your exercises so you can amaze your guests on Friday."

***

Friday afternoon, Daniel's stomach tied in knots no amount of massage could ease—if he could have convinced Clara to work on his abdomen. The thought of walking in front of his extended family filled him with dread. What if he fell? Besides, he walked so slowly people would think he'd made no progress worth mention.

He knew how much he had advanced. He'd gone from having useless legs to being able to stand on them and force his feet to move forward one slow step at a time. Would he ever be able to walk faster? To climb steps?

Not that he was complaining. After two years as an invalid, he welcomed the movement he had. But, to perform in front of a crowd scared him spitless.

He levered up and pulled his pillows so he was sitting. Using what he called baboon movements, he scooted back against the cushions. With the sheet off, he stared at his feet.

They appeared normal now. He appeared normal. This evening, he'd wear his old clothes and maybe his boots. He knocked on the wall separating his room from Clara's.

Soon, she popped her head around the door frame and grinned. "You summoned me with the royal bell pull, Your Majesty?"

"Will you help me pull on my pants and then my boots? I want to wear them tonight if I can walk in them." So far he'd only worn socks for his steps.

She hurried into the room and sorted through his belongings. "There is not much time to practice. Here is your pair of good pants. Oh, here are the boots. My, they are very fancy. Oh, I dislodged something."

Dadgummit, she picked up a book he'd hidden behind the boots in his armoire.

Advancing on him, she asked, "What is this? *A Thousand Unusual Facts to Amaze Your Friends: Be the Life of the Party.*" She held up the book as if she were showing it to him. "This is where you get all those weird items you tell me."

He grinned at her. "I told you I read them somewhere."

She laughed and returned the book to its hiding place. "Daniel McClintock, you are incorrigible. But, you have shared interesting things with me. I suppose I cannot be angry."

"I hope you're not. I need help getting these boots on my feet. After all this time, not sure they even fit."

"Start with the pants." She handed him his best pair of tan twill ranch pants.

He wriggled and struggled until he could fasten the pants at his waist. Not that they were too small. Quite the opposite.

Taking one boot, he tugged until his foot slid inside. Then, he pulled on the other boot. Damn, but it felt good to be wearing them again. He almost felt like his old self.

"Get rid of the nightshirt and wear these." She handed him one of his favorite shirts, a blue plaid, and his brown vest.

He tucked in the shirt.

"Try standing while I am beside you."

Tentatively, he rose from the bed and reached for the bars. The boots took getting used to again. He stumbled and without the bars would have fallen on his face.

"Do not be discouraged. Keep trying." Clara moved ahead and motioned him toward her.

He let his hands skim the bars without gripping them. "Darn it, I'm determined to go to the party wearing these clothes and these boots."

Carefully, he walked toward Clara. Another misstep sent him grasping the bars but he didn't fall. When he reached her, he slowly turned and she ducked under one bar to get in front of him again.

When he looked up, his parents stood in the doorway. Tears ran down his mother's face and his father appeared about to shed a few also.

Mama clung to Pa's arm. "I don't know when I've been so happy. You look like your old self, Daniel."

"Mama, don't you see how slow I am? This is not as I was. Still, after all this time I'm sure not complaining."

Pa took out his handkerchief and blew his nose. "Don't care if you move at a snail's pace, you're moving on your own two feet."

He kept walking, trying to go a little faster. "Not used to the boots yet and almost fell a couple of times. Want to wear them tonight."

Pa pulled out his pocket watch. "You have another hour at least. Don't overdo it, though."

Clara glanced at his parents. "Do not worry, I will not allow him to overtire himself. I do not think he would anyway for he wants to walk in tonight."

He grinned at her and at his parents. "Have to make an entrance, you know, like Gran."

With a last tear-filled glance from his mother, his parents left.

Clara watched his feet. "We will work for thirty minutes and then you should rest until people arrive."

"You dare give orders to royalty?"

"I most certainly dare. I will remind you that many kings die in their sleep."

"Yikes! She bites."

"I have never bitten one of my patients. Truthfully, I have wanted to pinch or slap a couple but I restrained my baser self."

He wiggled his eyebrows at her without stumbling. "Don't I know how strong your will to restrain yourself can be, having spent sleepless nights because of it?"

"So you say, but I shall remember your confession. Any sleepless nights you have had were due to not enough exercise during the day. Perhaps we will see you no longer suffer lack of sleep."

"Clara, neither of us could have withstood more than we've done. Surely not you."

Her chin went up in what he'd come to know as her defensive stubborn stance. "I am tough and strong. I was created for this job."

"Maybe, but everyone has endurance limits, even you."

When they had completed several circuits on the parallel bars. She checked her lapel watch.

"You must stretch out on the bed now. Do you want your boots removed?"

"No, will you return in time to comb my hair for me?"

"As soon as I hear someone arrive, I'll return. Get a cat nap. I hear they work for cats."

Chapter Sixteen

Clara strolled to her room deep in thought. Tonight her skills would be on display as well as Daniel's recovery. Soon he would not need her at all. She would still need him, but she would not stand in his way of finding a woman he could love forever.

The thought of him with another sent acid pouring into her stomach. She scrubbed a hand across her chest where her heart had split into shards. In its place, heaviness remained as of lead weights lodged inside.

She changed into the new dress Gran had made for her. She no longer felt festive, but she owed Gran for her generosity. Perhaps wearing something so lovely would boost her mood.

Rebecca knocked on her door. "Would you like help with your dress or hair?"

Clara smiled at her. "Both, please. I am not very good with hair. I can braid it or pile it into a bun."

"There, all fastened. Sit in the chair and I'll stand behind you. Do you have any pearls or a blue ribbon?"

"Neither."

"I'll be right back. Don't move." Rebecca dashed from the room and returned with a blue ribbon.

She spent at least fifteen minutes on Clara's hair. She stepped away.

"Now, see how lovely you look."

Clara rose and walked to the mirror. Her hair had never been more attractive. "That does it, you are my official hairdresser forever."

Rebecca giggled. "I'm glad you approve. I think I hear Josh and Nettie. Maddie's riding with Gran and Grandpa to help with the children. I'd better go see if I need to help with the baby now."

Before she left, Clara hugged her. "You are a wonderful girl and a good friend. Thank you for your help."

Clara got a fresh handkerchief and tucked it inside her cuff before she walked next door.

"Damn, you look good enough to eat." Daniel was sitting on the edge of his bed. "About time you arrived. I was going to summon you." He made a knocking motion in the air.

She curtsied. "I am her to do your bidding—at least, if it is what I think you should do."

Daniel rubbed the back of his neck. "Listen, we have to have a plan." He cleared his throat and his hands trembled. "I've been thinking. You wheel me to the parlor door but out of sight. I'll get up and walk into the parlor and you follow me with the chair. If I start to stumble, you push the chair under me. I'll need it anyway after a few steps."

She had never seen him so nervous. "That sounds like something that will work. You have only to signal me when you wish to sit down. Are you ready?"

He extended his hand palm out. "No… yes… I'll get in the chair in a minute but let's wait to go in until more folks have arrived."

She smiled at him, hoping she reassured him. "Of course, so you can make your grand entrance. Tell me, what did you think of *Huckleberry Finn?*"

He pointed his forefinger at her. "I know what you're trying to do but forget it. I'm too nervous to discuss anything. Why don't you kiss me? That always takes my mind off other things."

"On the contrary, it has been my experience that kissing puts other things in your mind. Nevertheless, I will give you a kiss. Just one and do not undo the nice hairstyle your sister painstakingly arranged." She leaned over to capture his lips.

He pulled her into his embrace with her between his legs. His kiss grew more passionate and she gave into her desire.

"Ahem."

Clara and Daniel broke apart. Embarrassed to be caught out kissing him, she knew she must be red.

Apparently unperturbed, Daniel stared at his brother who stood in the doorway. "You pop up at the durndest times."

Josh grinned. "Begging your pardon, Clara. Little brother, if you can pull yourself away from this lovely lady, Mama said Gran and Grandpa are here and it's time to come to the parlor."

Daniel transferred to the chair. "Okay, but we have a plan worked out for my entrance."

Josh shrugged. "I'm just the messenger. I'll go back to the parlor."

Clara pushed her patient to the hallway outside the parlor. Daniel took a deep breath and stood.

Clara leaned near and whispered, "You can do this."

He took slow steps and entered the parlor, with her following him. Furniture had been pushed to the walls and extra chairs brought in. People filled the room.

Everyone there stood and clapped. Dallas and Josh and Finn whistled. When he was about ten steps into the room, he signaled her and she positioned the wheelchair so he could sit down easily.

Houston toddled over to Daniel. "I ride, Unka Dan'l?"

"You bet, Houston, old buddy." Daniel lifted the boy onto his lap. He used his hands to move the chair back and forth.

Houston laughed hilariously as only a child can.

The boy's father captured Houston and held him high over his head where Houston squealed in glee.

Dallas took his son with him and sat beside his beautiful wife. "Give Uncle Daniel a break, okay?"

Houston looked adoringly at his father and nodded. "Break 'kay."

Gran dabbed at her eyes. "I'm glad we didn't miss that. Daniel, I'm so happy for you. You, too, Clara. I know you've both worked very hard."

Clara kissed Gran's cheek. "Your other grandsons helped a lot."

"I know and I thank Dallas and Josh, too." The older woman smiled through tears. "We have a wonderful family."

Brendan O'Neill stood. "I'd say this occasion calls for music. Are you ready, Aoiffe?"

His wife picked up a fiddle and put her chin on the rest. Her son Finn joined with his own violin. Mr. McDonald put a harmonica to his lips. Mac picked up what looked like a tambourine, but he beat it with a short stick with a ball at one end.

"What is that Mac has?" Clara asked Daniel.

"A bhodrân." He leaned forward. "Hey, Mac, didn't know you played the drum."

Mac nodded without breaking time. "Been learning this past year."

Brendan and Mrs. McDonald clapped in time.

Cenora leaned near Dallas and whispered. He nodded and took Kate from her. She gestured to Vourneen.

Cenora and her sister-in-law rose and danced with their backs straight and their feet flying. Rebecca joined them.

Clara clapped. She had seen Celtic dancing at Scottish cèilidhs but never any this fine, particularly no one as good as Cenora.

Clara leaned near Daniel so he could hear her. "Who is that seated beside Dallas?"

The man was about Clara's height and quite handsome. Silver threaded his black hair and his skin was light bronze. Although he wore clothes like those of the other men, his boots were soft rawhide and came up halfway to his knees.

"John Tall Trees is Cherokee Indian and is Dallas' maternal grandfather. He's moved here full time to be near his great grandchildren."

"Why does Gran glare at him?" When she looked at Mr. Tall Trees, Gran's mouth puckered like a prune.

"She wouldn't accept John's daughter as Houston's wife, so he went to live with John. She holds John responsible for Houston's death. That's ridiculous because John and his daughter saved Houston's life when he was robbed and left for dead."

"What a terrible thing to happen. And with him far from home."

Daniel nodded. "At the same time, John holds Gran responsible because if Houston and Gentle Dove had been living here, they wouldn't have run afoul of the gang of ruffians who killed them."

"He does not appear to glare at Gran. In fact, he has not looked at her."

"As far as he's concerned, she does not exist."

Petra, accompanied by Dr. Sullivan, chose to move closer beside Clara. She leaned near. "I brought my shoes and cap but I don't think I want to dance now that I've seen Cenora."

Kathryn yelled, "Cenora, please sing for us."

Rebecca fanned her face with her hand and plopped onto the floor beside her friend Maddie. Vourneen returned to sit with her children, who Maddie had cared for while their mother danced.

Cenora smiled and spoke to her family. They changed the tune and she sang "Believe Me If All Those Endearing Young Charms" then "Piping Tim of Galway" followed by "Green Bushes".

She curtsied to applause and gestured to her sister-in-law. "Stella and Nettie have lovely voices. Let's hear them."

Catcalls and cheers encouraged the reluctant sisters.

Stella and Nettie stood together and asked Aoiffe for "Barbara Allen" then sang "Greensleeves" *a cappella*.

Nettie said, "We'll close with 'Lavender's Blue' and let someone else perform."

Their voices blended perfectly to produce a wondrous sound. When they had sung three tunes, they curtsied and returned to their seats.

Clara clapped and leaned toward Daniel. "I have never heard better singers than these three women."

"What were you and your aunt whispering about? What were you scheming?"

She grimaced and shook her head. "Your family members are such accomplished performers, I do not have the nerve now."

"Hey, this is family. Go ahead."

She widened her eyes at him. "Says the man who was a nervous wreck earlier."

He reached around Clara to touch Petra's sleeve. "Time for you two to get your act going."

Petra nodded and pulled her shoes and hat from a bag beside her. "Clara, get your shoes on."

Clara sighed. "All right. I do not want to seem like a bad sport."

She hurried to her room and retrieved her shoes. She hadn't starched her cap so she didn't wear it. Besides, it would mess up her hairstyle. She made fun of herself. What a vain woman she had become.

When Clara returned to the parlor, Petra set the cap on her head and stood. "Clara and I will show you Dutch clog dancing. Fortunately for us, this is not as active a dance as that Cenora, Vourneen, and Rebecca did earlier."

Kathryn sat at the piano and stared at the wooden shoes. "Is that what's sometimes called clog dancing?"

Petra nodded. "Ja, do you know the music?"

Kathryn played a few notes. "Will that work?"

"Perfectly." Clara grabbed her aunt's hand and they moved to the center of the room.

Kathryn continued while Clara and Petra danced. Soon the other musicians joined the tune. Clara had to portray the man's part for her aunt, as the dance was intended for couples.

After a few minutes, Clara stopped. "You see how it goes now."

People clapped and she and Petra curtsied.

Austin called to a man across the room, "Tom, let's see a Cherokee dance."

The man shook his head and laughed. "Might make it rain."

Others joined in the mirth.

Dallas stood and glanced at his grandmother then at Mr. Tall Trees. "Come, 'gɹændfa, and we will dance together."

"I would not miss an opportunity to dance with my grandson." He turned to Mac. "Will you match out time with your bhodrân?"

Mr. Tall Trees and Dallas matched one another in a crouch. Houston ran to copy them. The older man chanted while he and his grandson turned this way and that, dipping as if stabbing something.

Clara thought Houston the most precious child she had ever seen. "Isn't Houston adorable trying to copy their movements?"

"I agree but look at Gran."

Gran's face scrunched in anger... and repulsion.

When the men stopped dancing, Dallas scooped up his son.

Mr. Tall Trees turned slowly. "Beware of the Cherokees. That was a war dance."

The audience clapped and laughed.

Emma stood. "Food's on the table. Help yourself and come back in here. I'll bring around drinks."

Rebecca stood. "I'll help, Emma."

Kathryn clapped her hands for attention. "We'll save the desserts for later after we've danced and heard more music."

Daniel leaned near. "Get me some of everything."

Austin held up his hands. "First, Brendan, would you give our blessing?"

Brendan puffed out his chest as he had done at the picnic. "I'll be pleased. Let's see if this one will do. As lovely as Eirin's rolling Hills, Fair as its lakes and streams, Joyful as it laughter, Bright as all its dreams, Lucky as its people, Happy as its leprechauns too, May that be how each and every day, Will always be for you. Amen."

Austin smiled at Council Clayton. "Would the English like equal representation?"

Council shook his head. "Not this Englishman. What about the Scots?" He grinned at Austin.

Together, the McClintock men said, "No."

Dinner was a massive feast. Each family had brought food, although Kathryn and Emma had provided more than enough.

When they were seated and balancing plates on their laps, Petra told Clara. "I only brought a cake. I should have brought more."

Beside her, the doctor asked, "Why? You don't think there's enough food?"

"Ja, you're right. I just saw some carrying in several dishes and I felt like the poor relative."

"Those were Kathryn's two sons and Finn who carried in so much. The others did not, yet look how much there is."

Daniel said, "Usually there's enough for at least three times this many people."

Clara speared a bite of barbecued beef. She hadn't added the sauce for fear she would drip on her new dress. "There is that much tonight. But there is a nice variety. I could not taste all of it because my plate was too full."

Daniel grinned at her. "That means you have to go back for seconds."

She nodded. "And while I am there I should get you another plate full, is that right?"

"You catch on quickly." He popped a bite of ham into his mouth.

Dr. Sullivan, who insisted she call him John, leaned forward. "Daniel, I can't tell you how pleased I am to see you so improved."

"Thanks for keeping me alive and finding Clara. Even though she isn't a man as her letter indicated, she has done a great job."

She nudged his arm with her elbow. "You will never forget that, will you?"

Petra frowned. "Is Daniel angry with you?"

Daniel laughed. "It's a joke, Petra. I was mad when she arrived because we'd expected a man. I didn't think a woman could do the job, but she bullied me and sure showed me how wrong I was."

Petra nodded, obviously still confused. "My English is not as good as Clara's. I miss a lot of jokes and… how do you say… local jargon?

Clara stood. "Shall I take your plate, Aunt Petra, or do you wish to get more?"

"No more for me. I am embarrassed at how much I ate but everything looked delicious. And, it was."

John stood. "I believe I'll have a bit more of that barbecue. Bachelors have to seize the opportunity for good food when we can." He glanced at Petra before walking toward the kitchen.

Clara widened her eyes at her aunt and leaned to whisper, "You should ask him for dinner. You're a great cook and he hinted."

Petra's eyes sparkled. "You do not think Hans would mind?"

"Definitely not." Clara took Daniel's plate. "More of everything or just specific foods?"

"No green beans or cabbage. Hold out for beef and a few beans and sweet potatoes and corn."

"Nothing green, little boy?"

He pulled a face but his blue eyes twinkled. "See, I said you catch on quickly."

When she returned to her seat, Mr. Tall Trees was talking to Daniel.

After handing Daniel his plate, she extended her hand to Mr. Tall Trees. "I am Clara Van Hoosan. Your dance was interesting. After you told us it was a war dance, I can see your motions mimicked sneaking through the brush, attacking, and slaying your enemies. Thank you for sharing your talent with us."

Surprise spread across his face. "My pleasure. I promise not to scalp you, at least not until Daniel is running on the path."

She laughed. "That is a relief. As annoyed as I am with my hair at times, I would like to keep it attached to my head."

He laughed. "I'll remember your request."

Petra nodded. "Me also, Mr. Tall Trees." She waved a hand dismissively. "Not the scalping part, although I would like to keep my hair. I meant I enjoyed your demonstration." She looked at Clara. "Is that the right word?"

He took her hand and patted it. "That will work fine. I am pleased to have met you ladies."

He bowed slightly and went to join Dallas and Cenora. At the same time, the doctor reclaimed his seat by her aunt.

Clara pondered her aunt and the doctor as a couple. If each of these two lonely persons found someone, the union would be wonderful. What would that do to the closeness she and her aunt had found if Clara moved away?

She wanted her aunt to be happy, but she'd visualized them remaining close. As in, Petra living wherever Clara worked. She sighed. Don't cross bridges before you reach them.

Chapter Seventeen

On Tuesday, the tenth, Clara rose early. Dressing quietly, she wondered whether Dr. Arnoldson would actually call. If so, what would she decide? Perhaps he would not come and she would not have to make a decision.

She tiptoed next door and peeked in. Daniel was awake and sitting on the side of his bed.

He looked up. "What, wearing your uniform to meet your important guest?"

She approached him. "Don't be mean, Daniel. I work in a uniform so why should I not wear one today?"

His eyes pleaded with her. "I don't want you to go. There's no need for him to come here."

"I did not have a way to contact him at his conference, you know that. Besides, I would like to hear his offer. No matter what my decision, knowing my options is always best."

"My offer includes a home with me and your own clinic. You'd be close to your aunt and my family. I know you like my family and they like you—even Gran likes you."

"I have grown quite fond of your family. Daniel, you know why I cannot agree. You do not know any other women your age. Not one."

His chin jutted out. "You don't trust me?"

"Of course I trust you. I know you would never violate your wedding vows. But, how do you think I would feel if we married and I realized you were more attracted to another woman? And, how terrible for you that would be."

"I won't be attracted to anyone but you. You don't have to parade a dozen women in front of me for me to tell you that."

She pushed the chair near him. "Come, get ready for breakfast. I hear Emma setting the table."

He scowled. "I am ready. I didn't sleep much."

"Daniel? You need your rest to rebuild your strength."

Sparks lit his blue eyes. "Yeah? I heard you pacing long into the night so don't lecture me."

She offered a weary sigh. "You are right. I have worried with this until I am exhausted yet still I cannot sleep. I wish the dratted man would arrive so I can be done with this decision."

After breakfast they worked with his walking between the parallel bars. Neither was talkative, which was unusual. Normally, this was a time when they joked and conversed on diverse subjects.

About ten, they heard a buggy approach. Each of them turned toward the window. A tall, good looking man stepped from the buggy and tied the reins at the rail.

Kathryn answered the doorbell. "Come in, Dr. Arnoldson, I'll tell Clara you're here."

"If I am not mistaken, she and her patient saw me from the windows."

In Daniel's room, Clara pushed the chair for Daniel to be seated. "Come with me, Daniel."

"Am I part of your pony show so you can impress him?"

"You know that is not the case at all. I thought you would want to meet him and listen to what he has to say."

He propelled the chair himself. "Lead the way."

They joined Kathryn and the caller in the parlor.

Dr. Arnoldson stood when Clara and Daniel entered. He was her height with sandy brown hair and brown eyes.

He took Clara's hand and bowed over it. "I am pleased to finally meet you, Miss Van Hoosan. I have heard remarkable things from your professors and from the local doctor."

He stretched his hand toward Daniel. "Nice to meet you also, Mr. McClintock."

Daniel remained in the wheelchair but shook the newcomer's hand. "Please be seated."

Emma brought in a tea tray, glared at the doctor, and left.

After winking at Clara, Kathryn served them.

"This is very kind of you. I am thirsty. I spent the night in your lovely town."

After they had had time to finish their refreshments, Dr. Arnoldson asked, "May I see the paraphernalia you've used?"

With a glance at Daniel, she stood. "Yes, if you'll follow me."

The four of them went to Daniel's room.

Clara gestured at the bars. "I brought this equipment with me in trunks and assembled it once I was here."

She gestured to the overhead hook. "That is for a harness Daniel wore until he could balance himself with only the parallel bars."

"And how did you force his feet to move?"

She chuckled. "By duck-walking backwards and moving his feet as he advanced on the bars."

"I see you must have a great deal of stamina."

"I have had several years to practice. I also used massage."

"On the legs?"

"Also on the shoulders and back as well. Using the bars is hard on a patient's shoulders especially. In addition, Mrs. McClintock is a healer and used massage to keep his lower muscles from deteriorating. Dr. John Sullivan and Mrs. McClintock worked together to prevent him from having pneumonia or heart problems."

"You must be very forward thinking, Mrs. McClintock."

She smiled graciously, but Clara sensed Kathryn did not like the doctor. "I use methods as old as time itself, Doctor Arnoldson."

He pulled a face. "Ah, quite so. Miss Van Hoosan, shall we go back to the parlor or would you prefer we speak in private?"

"There is no reason everyone cannot hear what you have come to say." She led the way back to the parlor and sat down.

Dr. Arnoldson smiled at each person in the room then focused on Clara. "I've heard remarkable accounts in town about your results. I hope you've given consideration to coming to St. Louis."

She inhaled deeply. "I have thought about your offer but I do not know any details."

He leaned forward and spread his hands. "Of course. My hospital board has given me permission to offer the following terms. You would be provided a modest home near the hospital. In addition to being in charge of the mechanotherapy department you would hire—and fire—your staff. Your starting salary would be six hundred dollars a year."

He must have taken her gasp to mean she disapproved because he hurried to add, "Of course, you'd get yearly raises." He leaned back. "Have I given you enough information to make a decision?"

"I believe so. As you can see, my patient is not yet fully recovered so I cannot leave at present."

Dr. Arnoldson pursed his lips. "We can hold your place until Thanksgiving but I must have an answer by then. We plan to be ready for patients on the first of January."

"That is generous of you. I will make a decision very soon."

He stood. "Since I won't be taking you back to St. Louis with me, I'd better rush and catch the afternoon train east."

Kathryn rose. "I'll see you out, Dr. Arnoldson."

***

Daniel felt gutted by a knife. Six hundred dollars a year plus a fancy hospital with a new wing for her and a house. He was shot down like the pigeon he was.

She sat staring into the distance. Probably saw visions of grandeur dancing in front of her. He sure couldn't compete. Except he loved her.

He took her hand. "Are you going to say anything?"

"He was disrespectful of Kathryn's ability. I didn't like that."

Thank heavens. "He was rude. Seemed too certain of himself but he sure offered you a lot of money."

She still appeared lost in thought, even though she spoke to him. "Even though I could hire staff, I would be working for him and his hospital board. I must think over everything." She stood. "Shall we get back to your exercises?"

He leaned back his head. "Clara, please take mercy on me. I'm so tired. Let me rest today and I promise I'll work twice as hard tomorrow."

Kathryn had come up quietly behind them. "I think you each need to take a day off. Clara, why don't you rest until lunch. If you wish, I'll take you to visit your aunt this afternoon?"

"You are always so kind, Kathryn. I would very much like to do that as soon as I get Daniel settled."

Dammit, he was not a baby. "Daniel can settle himself. I'm not the same age as Houston." He turned his chair and wheeled himself to his room.

***

Clara rode beside Kathryn in the buggy. "I did not mean to upset Daniel. I am just used to doing things to help him and I forget he can do most things alone now."

"He's just upset at the thought of you leaving. I admit we all are. You've become like family. You must know Daniel is in love with you."

"So he says. Kathryn, he has not been around a woman who is not a family member in over two years. How can he know how he feels about me? Once he is around women his age, he may forget about me."

"He has always known what he wanted, Clara. He knows all the available women in this area. I believe he genuinely cares for you." She shook her head. "Listen to me. I should not be trying to sway you either way. You need to make your own decision."

"Being swayed is very nice. I would cry if you were eager for me to leave. I think yours is the most wonderful family in the world."

"You're so kind. I love our entire family, too, especially now that Gran appears to have come around to being civil to me. Grandpa always was but Gran had picked out daughters of her friends for Austin and Houston."

"She could not have chosen a nicer daughter than you. I am fortunate to have met you. You do much good in the world."

"Sometimes. When a baby dies, I feel the loss as much and sometimes more than the parents."

"That would be hard. As is when I treat a patient that I know will never recover. There are many reasons, as I am sure you know, why the paralysis cannot be reversed."

"Which makes the triumphs that much sweeter."

They reached her aunt's home.

Kathryn remained on the buggy's seat. "I believe I will go visit Gran and Grandpa and let you and your aunt have time to discuss this offer together."

Clara climbed down. "Thank you, Kathryn. Tell the grandparents hello from me." She opened the gate and sauntered up the walk.

Petra opened the door before Clara rang the bell. "This is a welcome surprise. Come in and I will make tea."

Her aunt took her shoulders and turned Clara to face her. "*Mijn lieve meid*, what is wrong?"

"I do want to be your darling girl, Aunt Petra, but you may change your mind when you hear why I am sad. I have had a visit from that doctor in St. Louis and heard his offer."

"Then why are you filled with sorrow? Were the conditions so bad?"

"No, so good." She threw her arms around her aunt and wept on Petra's shoulder. "I do not want to go away. I want to stay here and marry Daniel."

"Ah, my poor Clara. Then that is what you should do. He is in love with you."

"Do you think he truly is or that he has not been around other women for so long?"

"You are not usually so unsure of yourself. Ah, but you are unsure of his love. I can tell you what I see. He loves you and he is smart enough to know his own mind. Does he not know all the women his age in town? If he wanted one of them he would not propose to you."

"I am so pleased you think so. When I get back to the house, I will tell him yes, I will marry him."

"And your clinic? What will you do about that?"

"Austin said he will give us forty acres of land overlooking the river on which to build a house and a clinic. That is enough for pretty gardens for the patients to have fresh air."

"But what will you use to build this place?" She slapped her hand against her forehead. "Ach, I still have not found the solicitor's envelope. I will spend all my time now looking through my papers."

"Shall I help you?"

"I would be too embarrassed for you to see my mess. Do not give up. I have made progress. I found your father's family Bible. I have not found mine or that of Hans' family yet."

Clara couldn't imagine the state of her aunt's papers if even a family Bible could remain hidden. No matter, she had more serious matters on her mind.

Petra took her hand. "I will ask Madame to make your wedding dress."

Clara shook her head. "I can wear the blue one. That dress is so pretty."

"Nonsense. I told you I have money. I received many guilders for our home yet homes here cost far less in dollars. Plus, I have the money Hans saved." A conspiratorial gleam lit her brown eyes. "I am not certain but I believe I am wealthy."

Clara couldn't resist teasing. "That makes you quite a good catch for John."

Petra gasped. "You should not jest about such things. Besides, he is a 'good catch' as you said."

"He seemed quite interested in you at the cèilidh. Have you seen him again?"

Her aunt blushed. "Yes, he has taken me to dinner and I have invited him here two times. He misses home-cooked meals."

Clara hugged her. "Aunt Petra, he can get excellent meals at the café but he enjoys being with you."

"I hope so." Petra laid a hand at her throat. "We are a couple of romantics, are we not?"

"Perhaps this is a good thing. Much better than being cynical."

Her aunt met her gaze. "Clara, how much did the man from St. Louis offer to pay you?"

"A 'modest' home to live in plus six hundred dollars a year. I do not know what he calls modest."

"So much?" She nodded. "He realizes your qualities and knowledge are valuable. If you are worth that to him, you are worth more to yourself."

Kathryn knocked at the open screen door. "May I come in?" When she was inside, she took Petra's hands in hers. "I am sorry to rush Clara away from you but the time is getting late."

Petra nodded. "We have had a nice visit."

When they were on their way, Kathryn glanced at Clara. "Did seeing your aunt help you?"

"She helped me find my own mind. Does that make sense?"

"Sometimes talking things over with someone we trust helps us see what we want to do."

"Please do not think talking with you did not help. Today I was able to speak with my two favorite women. I have made my decision. If Daniel still wants me, I will marry him. My aunt pointed out that he is too smart not to know his own mind."

"I can't tell you how happy that makes me, Clara. You have become like a daughter to me already."

"I hope Daniel has not changed his mind. He was upset with me when we left."

Kathryn laughed out loud. "You need have no fear of that."

Chapter Eighteen

Daniel wanted to pace but feared that was beyond him. After he tried without success to nap, he asked Rebecca to watch him walk the parallel bars. Every second he listened for the buggy.

Rebecca put her hand on his arm. "Don't go back down the bars. You've almost fallen twice. If you do, I can't get you up by myself. Go to bed until Clara comes back and you can concentrate."

He sat on the bed. "You're a brat, know that?"

She shook her forefinger at him. "You should talk. A grumpier man never lived than you've been today. I'm going where I'm appreciated."

"And where is that, the moon?"

The slamming door let him know her mood. Hell, everyone in the family was on edge. He lay on the bed and stared at the ceiling. Still couldn't sleep. Damn that Arnoldson.

At last he heard a buggy approach. He recognized Mama and Clara but they pulled around to the carriage house. At least he'd see Clara now.

Minutes later she rapped then entered his room.

He propped up on his elbow then sat up. She was beautiful and smart and all the things a good woman should be. He would never tire of looking at her or spending time with her.

Suddenly, he was so overcome with emotion he couldn't think what to say to her. He cleared his throat. "Um, is your aunt all right?"

"Yes, but she still has not found the solicitor's envelope. She did find my father's family Bible."

"How could she lose that?"

She giggled. "She still hasn't found hers or that of Hans and my mother's family. She said the van der Meers were knocking a hole in the wall separating the two houses as she packed and she panicked. She emptied all the papers, small paintings, photographs, and so forth into a trunk. She's sorting everything now."

He shook his head. "I thought you said she was organized."

"She always was. She and Uncle Hans lived in a flat when they were first married but soon moved into the house she just sold. She was moving on her own this time."

"And still mourning your uncle. That's rough."

She sat beside him. "You know what you asked me before?"

He wanted to shout hallelujah but he pretended to be dense. "You mean about pushing my wheelchair?"

She looked at her hands in her lap. "Daniel, don't make me say the words. The man should ask unless you've changed your mind."

He took the pins from her hair until her golden locks tumbled across her shoulders and back. "Clara Roos Van Hoosan, I love you with all my heart and soul. Will you marry me?"

"I will, Daniel McClintock. I love you with my heart and soul."

He swept her into his embrace. "My darling Clara. I was so afraid of losing you. I know that doctor has more to offer, but I love you more than he ever could."

"I think he is in love with himself. Besides, all I want is you."

"What changed your mind?"

"I did not change my mind about loving you. Your mother and my aunt each told me you are too smart not to know your own mind. I decided they are right. You are a smart man and if you say you love me then you do."

"How soon can we be married?"

"My aunt wants me to have a new dress and your mother and Gran will want to add to the plans. I do not really want to wait, but we should not be selfish. Your mother will get to plan Rebecca's wedding but my aunt has only me."

He stared into her eyes, "What does that mean?"

After biting her lip a moment, she said, "How about two months?"

He wanted to shout "too long" but he needed to be walking better. "I'll wait if I must. Today would be better from my point of view, but you're right. Others have to be considered. I suppose I'd better work even harder at walking unaided. As long as you love me, I can stand any amount of exercise to walk."

She caressed his face. "I would love you, Daniel, even if you never walked again."

"Shall I show you my painting?"

"Have you finished? I would love to see your latest work."

"If you don't mind, I'll use the chair." He stood to move to the wheelchair and then led the way to his easel.

He grinned at her. "This is a first." When he removed the covering, the painting was of her in her blue dress.

"Oh, Daniel." She couldn't hold back the tears. The painting was an idealized version of herself. Propped against the painting was a piece of paper. She picked it up and read.

"*My Someone*
Fair of face
And pure of heart.
She speaks
And the birds sing.
She laughs
And the creek flows.
She walks
With a grace
Unlike any other.
And she is to me,
As I am to her.
My someone.
My true love."

Happy tears streamed down her face. How could she have doubted his love?

"When did you write this poem?"

"Around a month after you arrived. I wanted to show it to you but I was afraid you'd laugh at me."

"Daniel, it's wonderful. How could you think I would not love these words? Is this painting the way you see me?"

"Honey, that's the way you look. Don't you ever use the mirror?"

"Not often. I would love one this size of you. Will you do a self-portrait?"

"I'd do anything for you."

***

Almost two months later, Clara stood in the parsonage dressed in white. She would have preferred a dress she could wear later, but let her aunt and Madam Thibodaux have their way.

Her aunt fussed with her veil. "You look like a princess. Someday you will have a new tower." She kissed Clara's cheek.

Clara's dress was ivory satin draped and trimmed in Honiton lace, which Madame said graced Queen Victoria's wedding dress. The veil was of the same lace with a cluster of silk orange blossoms fastening the top. A bow of the dress fabric attached just over the left breast. The high neck had a small fabric bow at one side. The sleeves were three-quarter with split cuffs turning back three inches over the sleeve.

Her gloves were white kid as were her slippers. She had planned her only jewelry to be her mother's locket but Daniel had presented her with a perfect strand of pearls and matching earrings.

Rebecca twirled slowly. "I feel like a princess in this bridesmaid dress."

She was wearing a pink silk taffeta gown trimmed in bows at the shoulders. The skirt fell in soft pleats trimmed in Brussels lace. The neckline was lower than Austin deemed proper but Madame assured him it was fashionable. He'd gone off grumbling, to the amusement of Rebecca and Kathryn.

Clara was too nervous to be amused or anything else but dazed.

Dear Lord, give Daniel the strength and stability to stand through the ceremony.

Kathryn handed her a bouquet of pink roses and white mums and a smaller one to her daughter. "Don't worry, Daniel made it down from the buggy just fine. He's sitting until time to begin the wedding. Josh will inconspicuously help him if he needs assistance. They practiced while Josh helped him stand so to others they'd look as if they were just shaking hands."

"He has worried the past month about being able to get into and out of the buggy without embarrassing himself. I'm glad he and Austin practiced each evening."

They had made his room theirs with her former room as a private sitting area. She wanted this day to be over so she and Daniel could be alone together in those rooms.

She hugged her aunt. "Aunt Petra, I'm so glad you chose pale lavender for your dress. Hans would approve. You are a lovely mother of the bride."

Petra beamed at Clara's terminology. "Ah, it is too early but you are right, Hans would not want me to wear black to your wedding."

"Remember to sit on the bride's side of the church. John should sit there also because he is the one responsible for me being here."

Her aunt blushed. "He said he will sit beside me."

Austin came to collect Kathryn and Petra and sent another disapproving glance at Rebecca's neckline. "I don't understand why Rebecca's dress couldn't come up high like Clara's."

Grandpa came into the parsonage. "Time to get to the church, Ladies. You two will mesmerize the crowd. Can't wait to see Daniel's face when he sees you, Clara." He chuckled. "Bet his eyes bug clean out of his head."

Rebecca started to pick up the back hem of Clara's dress.

Mrs. Hopkins, the minister's wife, took over. "You take care of your hem, Rebecca, and I'll help Clara. Such beautiful dresses. I don't think we've had a wedding this fine in town."

As Grandpa said, the sanctuary was filled to standing room. Her knees threatened to give way. If Daniel was as nervous, he would never be able to stand through the wedding. She clung to Grandpa's arm.

Mrs. Abernathy nodded and started playing the organ. Rebecca glided gracefully up the aisle. Grandpa and Clara followed three feet behind her. Through the sea of faces and murmurs, Clara was interested only in Daniel.

He stood at the front gazing at her. Love shone from his eyes. Josh stood very near Daniel, as if that was where the best man was supposed to be. Clara knew he wouldn't let his brother fall.

Pastor Hopkins smiled as he stood at the small lectern with his Bible open. Grandpa placed Clara's hand in Daniel's.

The pastor asked, "Who gives this woman in marriage?"

Grandpa winked at her. "Her aunt Petra Jaager and the entire McClintock clan." He left the altar to sit by Gran.

Sunshine illuminated the stained-glass window, sending colored beams of light flowing across the congregation. The glow that fell on Daniel and her was from the dove of peace. Clara counted that a good sign.

After they had spoken their vows, they turned and Pastor Hopkins presented them. "Ladies and gentlemen, I present Mr. and Mrs. Daniel McClintock."

She and Daniel had to go down two steps and that petrified her. Behind them, Josh walked almost on Daniel's heels. So only she and the minister could see, Josh pulled up Daniel's coat and grasped his pants' waist until they were down the steps.

Daniel exhaled when they reached the level aisle. She smiled at him and he returned her smile. Then, they walked slowly out of the church with Josh and Rebecca behind them.

Clara knew her new husband was tiring quickly. They reached the buggy and Austin was there ready to help. Quickly, he and Josh helped Daniel onto the seat then helped Clara sit beside him.

The plan had been for Kathryn to invite everyone to the McClintock home for a reception, delaying the departure of the guests in church until Daniel was in the buggy. Evidently Daniel and she had accomplished that goal. As Daniel snapped the reins and set the horse trotting toward the ranch, people poured out of the church building. Austin passed them on his horse.

Clara leaned back against the seat and linked her arm with Daniel's. "We made our escape and Austin will be there to help you down and into the house."

"You'll be surprised when you see what I have in my jacket pocket."

She delved into his pockets, one after the other until she found a folded envelope in his inside jacket pocket.

"Your aunt finally found the solicitor's letter."

Clara had waited too long to learn what her uncle had left her. She ripped open the correspondence and read. "Good heavens, Daniel, look at this."

He laughed. "I don't read Dutch. Interpret for me."

Converting guilders to dollars, she named the amount. "We have almost enough to build the clinic."

She folded it and replaced it in his pocket. "As the clinic's official business manager, you must be in charge of this."

"There's more, Love. Grandpa gave me a check." He reached into another pocket and pulled out a bank draft then handed it to her. "Don't drop that."

"Oh, Daniel. We have enough to build the clinic if we're very careful."

"We have others from Daniel, Josh, Pa, Petra, even John Sullivan. Seems like a lot of people want to help get that building up and going."

"This makes our day even more special. We are blessed and can begin building right away."

"Mrs. McClintock, it appears you're correct."

She rested her head on his shoulder. "That name sounds wonderful, Mr. McClintock."

"Glad you think so because you're stuck with it for the rest of your life."

"Promise?"

"Forever, my love."

Epilogue

Seven months later

Clara struggled to fasten her dress. "Oh, please help me with these underarm ties."

Daniel came to her assistance. "Why wear this if it's uncomfortable, honey? You're not hiding the fact you're pregnant."

She adjusted the folds of the blue brocade. "Aunt Petra had this made for me to wear today. I do not care that women in my condition are not supposed to be seen in public. I have no intention of missing the grand opening of our clinic."

He kissed her neck. "I love that you're in your 'condition' as you call it."

"Hmm, that is because our children are not kicking your ribs or jumping on your bladder. But, Kathryn assures me our babies are doing well. Help me with this caftan, please. Madame said it will drape and help me look less like an elephant."

He held the pale blue silk sleeveless garment. "Having twins is efficient of you."

"We will see how efficient I am when they arrive." She adjusted the folds, looked in the mirror, and sighed. "Who am I fooling other than myself? I am as big as our building."

He kissed her cheek. "You're radiant, my beautiful wife. Are you ready to go to the clinic?"

She set her navy hat on her head and gathered her gloves. "Let us go. In spite of the fact that I waddle when I walk, this is an especially happy day, husband."

"Only one more of many to come."

Dear Reader,

Thank you for choosing to read my book out of the millions available. If you'd like to know about my new releases, contests, giveaways, and other events, please sign up for my reader group at www.carolineclemmons.com. New subscribers receive a *Free* historical western titled *Happy Is The Bride*.

If you enjoyed this story, please leave a review wherever you purchased the book. You'll be helping me and prospective readers and I'll appreciate your effort.

Caroline

If you downloaded this book without purchase from a pirating site, please read it with the author's compliments. If you enjoy it, please consider purchasing a legal copy to support the author in writing further books. If you can't afford to buy it, please leave a review on Amazon or Goodreads – it really helps!

If you prefer reading western historical romance, you will enjoy being a member of the **Pioneer Hearts Facebook Group**. There you'll be able to converse with authors and readers about books, contests, new releases, and a myriad of other subjects involving western historical romance. Sign up at www.facebook.com/groups/pioneerhearts/

Read Caroline's western historical titles:

Mistletoe Mistake, sweet Christmas story set in Montana

Loving A Rancher Series for Montana Sky Kindle World: (sweet)
Amanda's Rancher, No. 1
The Rancher and the Shepherdess, No. 2
Murdoch's Bride, No. 3
Bride's Adventure, No. 4
Snare His Heart, No. 5
Capture Her Heart, No. 6

Patience, Bride of Washington, American Mail-Order Brides Series #42

Bride Brigade Series: sweet, set in Texas
Josephine, Bride Brigade book 1
Angeline, Bride Brigade book 2
Cassandra, Bride Brigade book 3
Ophelia, Bride Brigade book 4
Rachel, Bride Brigade book 5
Lorraine, Bride Brigade book 6
Prudence, Bride Brigade book 7

The Surprise Brides: Jamie, sensual, released simultaneously with three other of The Surprise Brides books which are: *Gideon* by Cynthia Woolf, *Caleb* by Callie Hutton, and *Ethan* by Sylvia McDaniel, each book about one of the Fraser brothers of Angel Springs, Colorado

The Kincaid Series: Sensual, set in Texas
The Most Unsuitable Wife, Kincaids book one
The Most Unsuitable Husband, Kincaids book two
The Most Unsuitable Courtship, Kincaids book three
Gabe Kincaid, Kincaids book four

Stone Mountain (Texas) Series:
Brazos Bride, Men of Stone Mountain Texas book one, Free, sensual Audiobook Available

High Stakes Bride, Men of Stone Mountain Texas book two, sensual Audiobook Available
Bluebonnet Bride, Men of Stone Mountain Texas book three, sensual
Tabitha's Journey, a Stone Mountain Texas mail-order bride novella, sweet
Stone Mountain Reunion, a Stone Mountain Texas short story, sweet
Stone Mountain Christmas, a Stone Mountain Texas Christmas novella, sweet
Winter Bride, a Stone Mountain Texas romance, sweet

McClintocks: set in Texas
The Texan's Irish Bride, McClintocks book one, Free, sensual
O'Neill's Texas Bride, McClintocks book two, sweet
McClintock's Reluctant Bride, McClintocks book three
Daniel McClintock, McClintocks book four, sweet

Save Your Heart For Me, a sensual romance adventure novella set in Texas
Long Way Home, a sweet Civil War adventure romance set in Georgia

Caroline's Time Travel
Out Of The Blue, 1845 Irish lass comes forward to today Texas, sensual

Contemporary Western Hearts Facebook Group
If you prefer contemporary western romance, you'll enjoy interacting with kindred souls and authors by becoming a member of Contemporary Western Hearts Facebook Group at www.facebook.com/search/top/?q=contemporary%20western%20hearts

Caroline's Contemporary Titles

Angel For Christmas, sweet Christmas tale of second chances, sweet

Texas Caprock Tales:
Be My Guest, mildly sensual with mystery, sensual
Grant Me The Moon, sweet with mystery, sweet

Snowfires, sensual, set in Texas
Home Sweet Texas Home, Texas Home book one, sweet

Caroline's Mysteries: (Texas)
Almost Home, a Link Dixon mystery
Death In The Garden, a Heather Cameron cozy mystery

Take Advantage of Bargain Boxed Sets:

Mail-Order Tangle: Linked books Mail-Order Promise by Caroline Clemmons and Mail-Order Ruckus by Jacquie Rogers, set in Texas and Idaho

The Kincaids, Books 1-4 in one set, sensual, Texas

About Caroline

Through a crazy twist of fate, Caroline Clemmons was *not* born on a Texas ranch. To compensate for this illogical error, she writes about handsome cowboys, feisty ranch women, and scheming villains in a small office her family calls her pink cave. She and her Hero live in North Central Texas cowboy country where they ride herd on their rescued cats and dogs. The books she creates there have made her an Amazon bestselling author and won several awards. Find her on her **blog**, **website**, **Facebook**, **Twitter**, **Goodreads**, **Google+**, and **Pinterest**. Click on her **Amazon Author Page** for a complete list of her books and follow her there to be alerted to new release. Follow her on **BookBub** for an alert to special deals.

Subscribe to Caroline's newsletter at www.carolineclemmons.com to receive a FREE novella of HAPPY IS THE BRIDE, a humorous historical wedding disaster that ends happily—but you knew it would, didn't you?

Thanks again for reading this book!

Manufactured by Amazon.ca
Bolton, ON

40942065R00096